# WHAT WE KNOW ABOUT HER



Krupa Ge is a writer based in Madras. Her reportage and cultural writings have appeared in *The Hindu*, *Firstpost* and *The New Indian Express*, among other Indian and international publications over the last fourteen years. In 2017, she won a Laadli Award for a weekly column on women in cinema, 'Ms. Representation'. She was awarded the Toto-Sangam Residency Fellowship for the year 2016, and was shortlisted for a Toto Prize in Creative Writing the same year. She is also currently dabbling in screenwriting. *Rivers Remember*, her debut book, was published in 2019 by Context. *What We Know About Her* (Context, 2021), her first novel, was longlisted for the JCB Prize for Literature.

## Praise for *What We Know About Her*

**Longlisted for the JCB Prize for Literature 2021**
**Shortlisted for the inaugural Women Writer's Prize**

'With an assured yet quiet voice Krupa Ge brings forth a novel that is rich and layered in domestic history. The book is also a mirror of how memory is constructed, that it is not just the milestones but the smaller nuances that make it memorable. With a voice that is whip smart, this book achieves a lot without being noisy.'

– The JCB Prize for Literature 2021 Jury

'Like the sea that borders its beloved city of Chennai, Krupa Ge's *What We Know About Her* is a work of tides. It's about the push and pull between love and freedom, friendship and aloneness, parents and children, music and noise. It vividly recreates the vast landscapes and small worlds of Chennai and Benares, worlds apart from each other but bound by a beautiful and particular modern Indian cosmopolitanism. Above all, it gives us a cast of characters so loveable and skilfully created that it hardly seems possible they don't exist. Here is a beautiful, ambitious debut, a book for everyone who understands that the past lives on in us, as a story and sometimes as a song.'

– Supriya Nair, Writer and Editor

'Krupa Ge was born to write and pin readers to the page. Her writing has spirit, presence, kickassery you want to bottle and snort. Few write about cities, people, and fallibilities, as well as she does.'

– Deepak Unnikrishnan, Author of *Temporary People*

'Really enjoyed reading this novel, which was reminiscent, in part, of Jennifer Makumbi's *The First Woman*, and also does one of my favourite things: telling a story through letters.'

– Gautam Bhatia, Author of *The Wall*

## *Reviews*

'Steeped in memory, social commentary, curiosity, and Carnatic music Krupa Ge's *What We Know About Her* is a fiction debut to be cherished.'

– Hansda Sowvendra Shekhar, *National Herald*

'Her debut novel is also charged by her confident storytelling, along with her ability to illuminate the intersections of caste, class and gender, especially in the lives of people who are loathe to reckon with these uncomfortable truths.'

– Somak Ghoshal, *Mint Lounge*

'When I think of how my life will be chronicled by future generations, I suspect (and hope) that some aspects of our lives will be deemed regressive in the same manner we regard those before us. Yet I also hope that the women in my life are not painted as victims, but in the rich shades Krupa Ge affords to her characters.'

– Gayathri Sankar, *Scroll.in*

'What Krupa Ge has achieved in her debut novel *What We Know About Her* is a depiction of reality without boundaries. There are only transitions in the form of prose. The novel defies classification; it has no lines. Yet, if you were to ask what the book is about the unequivocal answer would be, "women". The novel is a tender depiction of Indian women and their agency.'

– Percy Bharucha, *Hindustan Times*

'... unputdownable. I finished the book so fast, like I was devouring a tasty burger, one big bite after another ... Kudos to Ge for creating a bunch of likeable characters. The story moves like a gently flowing river, aided by the cool breeze of Ge's writing.'

– Rachna Chhabria, *Asian Age*

'Krupa Ge's debut novel is about making journeys. The journey of unravelling the truth, the journey is in time too, from the past to the present and back, especially through the letters written by the protagonist—Yamuna's grandmother to her grandfather. It is a journey even in terms of geography, particularly between the two cities which have their own character in the novel—Chennai and Banaras. She depicts the journey of the struggles of the women … belonging to three generations … Consequently, it also becomes a journey of the self.'

– Jennifer Monteiro, *The Book Review*

**Praise for Krupa Ge's debut non-fiction book,**
***Rivers Remember: The Shocking Truth of a Manmade Flood***

'[An] absolute must read. Well written and carefully researched, it brings home the full horror of the catastrophe. This is what the future holds for many cities around the world.'

– Amitav Ghosh, on Twitter

'Weaving together Krupa's own harrowing experience of the floods with that of others whose lives were forever changed, *Rivers Remember* also meticulously traces the why and how of what happened. Taut and incisive, this is a cautionary tale that serves to remind us we can only abuse nature so much, while telling the larger story of how urban planning works across India.'

– Anita Nair

'Chennai's history, tradition, culture and people are vital to the idea of a rich, diverse India. […] Combining historical documents, first-person accounts, interviews and government reports, this painstakingly researched book makes an important contribution to keeping such memories alive.'

– Arvind Subramanian,
Former Chief Economic Advisor

'A powerful book that speaks truth to power, and such important reading in a city where life is wedded to its water history.'

– Meena Kandasamy, on Twitter

'The Cooum, Adayar and Kosasthalayar rivers carry within their dark waters the future, present and the past of their city—Chennai. In December 2015, that city drowned. From deep within those unforgiving waters, Krupa Ge recovers stories, memories and truths […] Through this telling, she warns us of a dystopian future where 2015 comes to stay, even as the death knell gets louder.'

– T.M. Krishna

## *Reviews*

'It is this job of contributing to the cultural memory of the disastrous Chennai floods of December 2015 that Krupa Ge's book does with deceptive simplicity and barely suppressed rage.'

– Nisha Susan, *Firstpost*

'I was more struck yet by how simply and movingly it documents something that's very little written about—our own ordinary, shifting, inadequate but real emotional battle to come to terms with what is happening to us.'

– Supriya Nair, *Mumbai Mirror*

'Ge's work is that rare slow reportage that could be instructive to multiple stakeholders in present-day India if they allowed it to be. It's one of the strongest works of narrative non-fiction to come out of India recently—elevating reportage with nuanced, even-keeled writing that tells the story of a place as much as of an event.'

– Urvashi Bahuguna, *Open*

'In a powerful, poetic narrative that moves between individual stories and the story of a city's drowning, Ge describes the unspeakable hollowing out of lives.'

– Uma Mahadevan Dasgupta, *The Indian Express*

'A touching story about the people who suffered, rendered, at times lyrically, poetic as a gently flowing river, and then, with cold facts, cold as the waters that swirled the muck into homes.'

– Ramya Kannan, *The Hindu*

'Piecing together the collective failure of the authorities to protect its inhabitants from an avoidable tragedy in Chennai, Krupa Ge brings to life the agony of the trapped in a touching account of those unforgiving waters of the city rivers, relentless in reclaiming their rights over their course in *Rivers Remember.*'

– Sudhirender Sharma, *Hindustan Times*

'Elegantly blends reflections, reportage, slices from history and moving personal accounts of several of those who suffered the tragedy.'

– M.R. Venkatesh, *The Asian Age*

'For the sake of creating awareness of ground realities among the people, may the tribe of those nameless auditors who studied the Chennai Floods 2015 under the CAG of India and wrote an eminently valuable stand-alone report, as well as of authors like Krupa Ge, grow.'

– Himanshu Upadhyaya, *Citizen Matters*

'This book holds valuable lessons for people everywhere.'

– B.R.P. Bhaskar, *The Tribune*

'Amartya Sen has asserted in his writings that famines cannot occur in countries with a free press. After reading Ms Ge's book, we can also assert that floods cannot occur in a country with a free press—and the absence of one makes us vulnerable.'

– Uttaran Das Gupta, *Business Standard*

'*Rivers Remember* is a book that every Chennai vaasi must read—Krupa's fierce love for the city shines through its pages. It leaves one feeling uneasy, with the author's meticulous, data-backed research warning us that the root causes of the flood still hang over our heads like the Sword of Damocles.'

– Varsha Venugopal, *Madras Musings*

# WHAT WE KNOW ABOUT HER

*Krupa Ge*

cntxt

First published in hardback by Context, an imprint of Westland Publications Private Limited, in 2021

First published in paperback by Context, an imprint of Westland Books, a division of Nasadiya Technologies Private Limited, in 2022

No. 269/2B, First Floor, 'Irai Arul', Vimalraj Street, Nethaji Nagar, Allappakkam Main Road, Maduravoyal, Chennai 600095

Westland, the Westland logo, Context and the Context logo are the trademarks of Nasadiya Technologies Private Limited, or its affiliates.



ISBN: 9789395073615

10 9 8 7 6 5 4 3 2 1

This is a work of fiction. Names, characters, organisations, places, events and incidents are either products of the author's imagination or used fictitiously.



Typeset by SÜRYA, New Delhi
Printed at Nutech Print Services-India

*For Swaroop*

*Kasiki poyyene neevalane, Kasiki poyyene*

(To Kashi I went away because of you, To Kashi I resigned)

—Kshetrayya, seventeenth century

# Contents

# WHAT WE KNOW ABOUT HER

# 1

# To Banaras

I was going to see my grandfather about a matter of inheritance. I had every intention of inheriting my home, sparse and secluded as it was. It didn't look like I would succeed, but I was determined to try.

The train was between stations, somewhere in the middle of small-town silence. A comforting, clove-scented fog settled inside my head as I lit up the first cigarette of my trip at the door of the coupé.

My mother is not an easy woman. This long-drawn fight over my claim to the house that stood on our ancestral land was necessitated by her need to give things away. She wanted to donate this house to some godforsaken NGO now. Amma was not like those irritating commies you ran into on Twitter: well meaning, politically correct, snarky and cutting people to size. The ones that turned up to work stoned, or wrote things like 'rest is revolution' and 'self-care is work' on their social media. She wasn't the kind you would identify as a jholey-wali. Amma was old school; a hardened, hit-the-streets, hold-that-flag-up kind of commie. A trade union lawyer who took after her leftist father. She dressed like nothing special—cotton saree, a maroon pottu on her forehead, wedding chain, toerings, her hair oiled and braided. She lived her ideals, didn't dress up for them as if they were something other than life itself. I admired her and her work. But her ideals had begun to encroach upon every little comfort I could access. Now she was after the place I'd called home since I was eighteen.

What kind of parents leave their city-bred, teenaged daughter alone in a mofussil town to take care of an old home that was under repair? At that time, my brother was studying in Bangalore and my father was travelling to the smaller cities every week on work. Amma was needed in Chennai, she was busy, busy, busy. So I, all of eighteen, was in charge of our old house in Chengalpattu. At first, I only went across on the weekends, but soon after I graduated, my parents tore down our crumbling ancestral house and built a new one. That's when I was asked to stay close by in a cheap, dingy women's hostel and help the maistry.

From afar, my house looks bucktoothed and genial. The windows on the first floor make up the eyes, and when you close one of them, it looks like the house is winking at you. The main door and the beam on top are the house's mouth. The balcony that runs right across the middle has plants that I've never been good at looking after.

When the new house was ready, Amma asked me to pack up and come home to Madras. She wanted to rent it out. I didn't because I was upset. How dare she use me like a watchman? If she thought I was old enough to oversee its construction, she had to know that I was old enough to make that home mine. It's not as if she paid for the repair work, or the new house, she hadn't even paid for my stay. My grandfather had sponsored it all. So I stayed put as nights turned to weeks and then years. Every once in a while, my mother recruited someone from the family to camp out in Chengalpattu. To threaten, cajole or blackmail me into leaving.

Amma had failed then. She'll fail now too.

I have often wondered if she really is my mother. There are no pictures of her pregnant with me. I know, I've looked. The thought really came upon me because of my brother. When I was seven or so, he started calling me Jujube Kumar. He said I came from a village called Jujube, deep in a forest, where people lived in circular homes, and that our mother bought me from the market in exchange for a few sprigs of curry leaves. She brought me home in a basket to be his pet animal, my brother said. He'd point to my deep jaggery brown, hairy arms and say, 'See how dark you are,' and then point to his own fair arms and say, 'See how I am like Amma, fair.' I would laugh, never giving him the satisfaction of a win. But deep inside, seeds of doubt had begun to appear, and I'd conducted tests on my mother over the years to see if she really had me. There was no Google, internet or computer in our homes and lives back then or I would have called his bluff right away.

When Amma sent me away, this suspicion grew very strong. It was only after I refused to move out of the Chengalpattu home that she told me why she'd sent me there. My father had maxed out his credit card and had no money to pay the bills. He had gone on a long leave of absence from his government job, and had started to work for a multi-level-marketing company, to sell soap, toothpaste and hair oil. The first month when he made no money, he started to use his credit card, and by the fifth month, he was like an addict, swiping wherever he went. Burly, intimidating men, collection agents, would show up at odd hours, Amma said, to collect credit card dues. One of these men, she said, made an unsavoury remark about daughters and wives, and the kinds of 'occupation', whoring one presumes, they must pursue to pay their bills instead of cheating creditors. That nameless asshole had changed the course of my life, words can do that. He was why I was sent away.

There were other reasons too that I was fleeing to Banaras from Chengalpattu. One of them was in my hands; a yellow-brown, ink-stained letter my grandmother wrote in her youth to my thaatha. The romance it hinted at took me by surprise. Why had I never asked the women in my family how and if they loved? We didn't talk to each other about love, come to think of it, ever. We lived as if love had nothing to do with us, all of us, daughters, wives, aunts, grandmothers and grandaunts. We lived in a world where everything, like marriage, was arranged to cause the least confrontation between people. Yes, even flag-waving leftists had arranged marriages within 'the community' in our family. A family of Telugus and Tamils, intermingled indistinguishably, speaking a language of its own that was neither here nor there, of migrants who criss-crossed the lands over hundreds of years, before states in independent India took on linguistic identities.

'What people are your in-laws?' you'd be asked, if you went to invite a relative to your wedding. No one used words like upper caste or brahmin in our educated homes. It was always subtler than that. You'd have to give them the sub-caste or regions your would-be's ancestors hailed from. Velanadu, Mulakanadu, Palakkad, Thengalai, Vadagalai and the like. Love marriages, especially with those from outside the community, were rare, and invites to those weddings were always prefaced by hand-wringing and long explanations from parents on how hard they'd tried to stop the wedding from taking place.

Just as I reached for my second cigarette, the near-idyllic silence was suddenly lost. Loud men got off the train, hanging on to railings like monkeys, walking up and down on tracks that glittered like hot black diamonds. Talking on their cell phones, looking important. I didn't want any attention from them, so I returned to my seat.

I ate through the rest of the journey out of sheer boredom. My cell phone buzzed every now and then with spam. I didn't speak to anyone except strangers on Twitter.

Outside, in pits of sand that were once a lake, two men sat unspeaking. Smoking beedis. Plastic bags posing as cranes drove unwelcome, thieving birds away. In some places, the grass grew so tall I could see nothing beyond them. Save for minarets in pistachio green, palm tree heads swaying under the spell of a brief breeze and strange thorny, pointy trees that never grow in cities. On a narrow trail, two boys cycled, carrying a large stainless steel tiffin box each. Further down, women were working in fields.

Travelling alone through nondescript places in a somewhat empty train, falling asleep to the chugging, getting off at random stations to buy food, reading undisturbed. All the romance of it is gone when you need to go to the bathroom. Especially if you're on your period. I had to resort to acrobatics in there. What to hold, where and how to wash, where to chuck my pad.

An older white woman in kurta-pyjama made an about-turn after stepping into the Indian toilet. 'It's what hell must smell like,' she said. But you gotta go when you gotta go.

There will always be a big positive to train travel: Higginbotham's at the Chennai Central, my station sanctuary. Buying a book from the store before getting on a train was among the few rituals I performed with devotion. I picked up my first Sweet Valley University as a giggly, nervous teenager on a class trip to Coorg; *Archies* on summer vacations; and there were those *Tinkle* digests with Suppandi and Chamataka. I devoured countless *Gokulam*s on trains, lying on my mother's lap. The 'one shelf for fiction, one for non-fiction and ten for self-help' kind of bookstores at airports would never match up.

This time, though, the book lay neglected. I spent most of my two days on the train reading my grandmother's letter, and then re-reading it. I'd have to ask my grandfather about it, ask if he had more letters from her. I deleted all my messages and emails as soon as I read them. I didn't want to leave behind anything I'd written. Memories are what photographs are for. Correspondence is different. They are short in love and long in hate. At least that's what I thought then. So this letter, all this talk of love from the matriarch was beguiling to me. My grandfather wrote a lot as well, but I didn't think much of his writing. Men wrote, I took that for granted. I didn't think women would leave their letters lying about. Especially back then. I thought they'd have them destroyed, for if you said one wrong thing, you could get caught in the quicksand of pettiness and scandal.

## 2

11.2.1940
Chingleput

Dearest,

Greetings. Are you well? All are well here. Nana conveys his regards, and Amma her blessings to you.

Over the last week I have slowly learnt to slip back into the old ways of this large house. Madras, on some days now, seems like a distant dream. Even my routine has changed here. Nana insists I drink bed coffee.

You can wash your mouth later. Coffee is hot, come, come, my father says, every morning. Who can say no to that?

My mother thinks that I sit at the entrance in the evenings hoping you will magically appear. She does not want me to sit alone in the thinnai. On gloomy, rainy nights, I don't want to be inside. Like winged termites that come for mud lamps in alcoves, restless, looking for light before the rains, I sit outside, waiting for something to happen. Maybe, as she says, for you to come and see me.

The only change from my life before marriage here has been Amma's pronouncement that I will be given a break from kitchen work. After the humiliation of my first miscarriage, the gossip and ostracising that came with it from my father's sisters, I was worried about announcing my pregnancy. Amma asked me to keep it under wraps too for fear of the evil eye. A day after I arrived, I was just about to scatter cow dung water to cleanse the porch for the morning, when I felt something on the floor: it was a dozen reddened lemons and betel leaves.

Amma cried to Saapati Amman, and offered milk to the ant hill.

She said the same thing all day, praying to the goddess. This is the third time we have found something like this. Someone wants to bring down a dark curse on this house. Help me counter their black magic. You are my only protector, Amma, save my daughter!

My mother thinks it is the handiwork of a kept woman of one of my uncles or grandfathers. That or some man who's lost money to them while gambling. She's convinced they are trying to bring death into this house. I told her it was an unreasonable leap in imagination. She wouldn't listen.

Anyway, the second Manian mama found out I am with child, news spread wildly, the way the karepaku plant goes, wherever the wind takes it. Mama was poking around the kitchen, where he should not have been, and he heard Amma tell one of my aunts about my morning sickness.

Now and then, though, I feel as if I am playing the part of a grown-up. In my heart I know, just as well as you do, that I am just a girl. Same as the one who came to you, shaking, fear announcing its presence in every part of her being, the day I moved into your home in patnam. I do not know how to explain this to the others here, but Amma assures me that this is true of all women. And that, eventually, everyone did grow into real women.

Amma was braiding my hair when she told me this: you will become me. Like I became my mother. One day you will look in the mirror and search. In vain. You would have disappeared. And your mother's face will smile back at you. You can change your hair now. Wear your bindi differently. Never wear your saree the way I wear it. Leave the tiniest bit possible at the end as pallu, not long and winding like I do mine. Or wear only glass bangles and not lac. But a day will come when your hair will be worn the way I wear mine now. When you will tie your saree the way I do mine. When you will wear only lac bangles. When you rummage through my ruins long after I have gone, looking for my remnants, you will find them only in the mirror, in your own reflection, she said.

When I arrived, my mother too was pregnant. Four months at that time. We would exchange notes on our morning sickness routines. Hers was always worse than mine. It makes me guilty now to think that I found comfort in it. A few days in, Amma pointed to her womb and threw her hands up in resignation: your brother has bled away. She did not seem upset when she said it.

I'm nauseous all day long. In the little time that I have at hand, feeling okay, I have been learning to sing from my sister. Lalitha has taught me two of my father's favourite songs. *Annapurne Visalakshi* and *Marugelara.* I tried singing them again this morning with Lalitha, but I cannot sing as well as her. When she sings, it is as if I am listening to the sounds of a waterfall, natural, unhindered, with seemingly unending depth and expanse. Her voice has the same effect as honey does on the quartz lingam in our house. It hits you and moves along its course, leaving behind a trail of sweetness that attaches itself to your soul. In the last year alone, she has given twenty public performances. I saw the dates in her diary. At temples in Chingleput, with violin and mridangam accompaniments,

Mahila Samajam and at three different venues in patnam. All thanks to you, she says. She's grateful to you and she makes it known, my little Lalitha.

She has grown into a star in town, that is certain. I see a new light in her eyes. And as she walks behind Amma on the streets, when we go to the temple, everyone waves at her. At the temple, the priest always asks her to sing and we all receive special treatment. Lalitha sings readily whenever anyone asks. In school, she tells me, she has won an embroidery competition, stitching with her left hand.

There is some good news I wish to share with you. Today, Mr and Mrs Easwaran and their party, who had heard Lalitha sing at the Trichinopoly hall, came home. They came dressed as they would for a wedding. The women decked in gold jewellery, looking like dark apsaras holding large brass platters. Amma was taken aback by the suddenness of it all. This shock soon gave way to utter joy. She went out to see what was happening when a cousin came running in and told her that a huge party was arriving to ask for Lalitha's hand. The crowd, he said, had the groom too.

Lalitha was shepherded into one of the rooms behind the kitchen, and all the other young girl cousins were sent upstairs to the store room. I helped Lalitha get ready. She went quiet in fear.

I am very scared, Akka, she kept saying. I cradled her in my arms and asked her not to worry. I told her that this was going to be just like her concert in Madras. Remember how she was scared at first, but really enjoyed performing later on? She did not say much after that. I braided her hair tightly, she hates it when I do that but didn't protest much. My cousin quickly strung together jasmine with kanakambaram and marugu from the backyard. Lalitha prefers jaathi malli blooms in long muzhams flowing freely from her hair, but we couldn't find any, so we stuck the Congress colours in small bits on her hair messily. Amma took out her gold chain and I took off my glass bangles. We pushed all of the bangles onto one of Lalitha's hands; the other one, Amma said, Lalitha would have to keep under her saree. Hidden.

Amma was very quiet, except for that one instruction she gave Lalitha: they know about your missing ring finger, let me assure you. But there is no need to flaunt it.

I felt bad but did not say anything. Lalitha seemed frozen. She did not even let out a sound. After what felt like forever, the chatter in the courtyard grew smaller and they asked me to bring the bride-to-be. The boy was seated on the old swing near the courtyard, and his father and uncles on chairs next to him. The women from both sides filled up the entire courtyard. This wedding is going to be a much grander affair than ours, I can already tell. Lalitha walked in and touched the ground.

We heard her sing in Tiruchi and knew immediately that she was the one for our family. We all sing, you see. But not in public. When the prospective mother-in-law made this announcement, my father's face fell.

My mother did her best to comfort them. Of course. All this singing in public can't go on once she is married. We know that. It's just her father's whim for now. She will sing at home for you and that's more than enough, Amma assured them.

The mother-in-law-to-be seemed very impressed with Amma's promise. Lalitha did not look up. And if she was angry or disappointed, she did not show it. I was proud of her resolve. Within every tantrum-throwing girl lurked her mother's voice, instructing her to hold it all in until the time was right to let it out.

While the adults snacked, the boy's father asked Lalitha to sing. The boy seemed bored. He looked as if he would rather be someplace else. As if he was being forced into doing all this. Based on their expressions and complete lack of interest, I thought that perhaps they were perfect for each other. Lalitha and Venkatesan. An old woman from the boy's side scoffed at our coffee, as if we had offered her contraband, and demanded buttermilk.

Without looking up, her voice confident as ever, Lalitha sang. She kept time with her right hand. Amma was disappointed that Lalitha had forgotten (or ignored) her instruction again. They watched her hand for a while. They gasped every time Lalitha kept time with her toe, when she could not keep time with her missing ring finger. But as her voice rose higher and higher, they too seemed to rise above that detail and hear her. We all did. It was marvellous. Lalitha's talent as a musician lies not just in singing but also in choosing the perfect song for the occasion. That Arunachala Kavirayar felt most natural, as if it were a song tailor-made for this occasion.

*Yaaro, ivar yaaro, enna pero.*

It brought her not just applause but something unusual. A request from the thus far reclusive groom-to-be. The crowd broke into loud laughter and applause when he asked, 'Can you sing another song?' And without hesitation, before anyone could register a protest, Lalitha sang. *Eppadi manam thunindhado.*

We all took it as a sign that this match would work. Lalitha continued to sing as the men exchanged tamalapaku. They came prepared with a ring. Like a real lady, my Lalitha was given a ring to wear on her left hand. I saw the weight lift off Amma and Nana's shoulders.

Later, when I helped her out of the saree, Lalitha hugged me and cried.

'His face, did you see it, Subbu? It bears no semblance of kindness. When he asked me to sing again, he didn't sound like he liked my music. He sounded as if he were the master and I his performing monkey. I will have to dance to his tunes 'ka. Please. I don't want this.'

She was being unfair and I told her she was. Why couldn't she see what we all could? They didn't even bring up her hand. I angered her though by bringing it up.

I thought you were on my side. I thought you would support me. You always have. Why have you changed? You have turned into Amma, she said and then cried. I slapped her lightly. Gave her a kiss on the cheek, wiped her tears and fed her hot rice with ghee and pappu chaaru. She will get over it. The little joker that she is, do you know what she asked?

Did you see his moustache, Subbu? Exactly like Hitler's. Why would any sane man do that?

Ever yours,
Subbu

# 2
# Hesitation

The first time I alighted at Varanasi Junction, in 2009, the announcer had said, 'Madhraas se aanewali gaadi'. Madhraas, I'd giggled to myself.

Madras was a lot of things to a lot of people. For me, it was sometime in the Nineties. It was that couple making out in Marina beach, not giving a fuck about who was watching, on a white-hot day in the shadow of catamarans. It was the humble sundal by day, just-boiled channa, shaved raw mango and peas, and hot chilli bajji and spicy chutney by night. It was summer days and naps, and waking up to ripe mangoes. It was a white shirt paired with blue denims. Comfortable. Classic.

What would the staccato female voice announce now? Anti-climax: she said the train had come from Chennai Central. It will be a while before she figures out they've changed the name of the station too. My train was actually arriving from Puratchi Thalaivar Dr M.G. Ramachandran Railway Station.

It was late evening and very cold outside, and the platform smelled heavily of pee. It hadn't occurred to me to wear a sweater; it hadn't occurred to most of us on that train that it would be that cold outside. My hands were numb, and according to my phone, it was around eight degrees just then. I had never been to Banaras in winter before, and was beginning to wonder if this was all a mistake. Madras winters were a pleasant 24 degrees at its coldest. And even that was monkey-cap weather for many of us. I wrapped my dupatta around me like a shawl and walked towards the exit.

Through the train journey, I'd been thinking of Thaatha's words. 'A pilgrimage changes us. It removes us from the comfort of the familiar and reminds us that, with each passing second, we are hurtling towards uncertainty, and, thus, of what's important.' He'd said that to me when we were travelling to Allaha—, ahem, Prayagraj.

When I asked Amma why my grandfather dumped atheism for spirituality, she just said, 'We don't really talk about his spirituality. It's a very dry subject, no?' As if I had asked her about a towel hung out to dry in rainless Madras.

The sun was on its way down, and the calm sky, the colour of parijatham stalk, made me homesick. My Chengalpattu home has a large, twisty tree. The smell of parijatham flowers early in the morning as they dropped over the previous day's kolam, like little pearls, was intoxicating.

Just outside the station, a little girl was chasing a cycle tyre with a stick. Dragging my trolley suitcase along, I began to walk up to her. Soon, I was jogging to catch up, and just as I did, she looked at me and said, 'I will pose for a photo if you give me a chocolate.'

I told her I was not a tourist looking for pictures of kids with runny noses acting cute, and that I was visiting Thaatha. The girl clearly hadn't recognised me. She thought I was asking for directions and ran down the road, beckoning me. Her mother worked for my grandfather. I hadn't called him. I hadn't even planned on coming here. There was a lot going on, and I'd just booked a tatkal ticket to see him on a whim.

There was the matter of the house, of course. I'd also fought with the man in my life. Sundar and I were in that place in our relationship where I was no longer happy to see his face. We both wanted more or less the same things. I wanted less, and he more, of the relationship or whatever it was that we had. I needed some time off to sort out the scramble in my head.

Thaatha's house looked like it had received a fresh coat of paint recently. I wasn't sure why. Was he planning on giving this one also away? The two entrance doors were wide open as always. On the left door, an aluminium board read K.V. Kannaiya.

My great grandfather had built this house of greens and browns. All the doors and windows green, and every piece of furniture in the house a deep brown—the planter's chairs with their always-dusty cane bodies, the old beams that ran through the ceiling, the rickety staircase that wound its way up, the wooden flooring in the first storey. A few feet from the entrance, the courtyard was sun-lit through the year. In the middle of it were remnants of a dead plant in a cement pot, with alcoves for lamps that no one lit. Beyond was a sparse seating area, with uncomfortable mango-wood chairs and a large teak swing. On the walls beyond were photographs. They made up a haphazard family tree. Everyone on that wall was somehow related to me.

Looking at the photos of my inbred, dead ancestors—until Thaatha was old enough to call the shots, everyone married cousins as was the custom—you could neatly divide the gene pool into two categories. You were either dark, with smoothly aligned teeth, or you were fair and had terrible teeth. I was the exception, the colour of strong filter coffee, with a small case of buck teeth. I cupped my hands in front of my mouth whenever I laughed, thanks to that buck-teeth gene.

Between those black-and-white photos were pictures of gods from old cardboard daily sheet calendars that hung on to the wall long after the years had rolled on, leaving them behind. I looked for Thaatha in various rooms around the courtyard and found him in the one on the right corner, where the setting sun emptied out the last of its glow. He was reading.

'Arerey, what a surprise. Welcome home, O busy one,' Thaatha said in a tone that at once made me feel guilty for all the calls missed and visits skipped, as well as adored and young. Thaatha, looking sharper than I remember, at ninety-six, was sitting on the floor. I stayed in his arms for a few seconds. Taking in his soft kurta, the scent of his vibhuti and the slight coldness of his old arms, crinkled, like the outside of a whole copra. I could feel my own smile as he patted my back gently, awkward in the embrace that he never could get used to. He then planted a kiss on my cheek.

The little girl, sans tyre and twig, tugged at my kurta.

'Yamuna, don't give that Mallika any chocolate,' Thaatha said, pointing his walking stick at her. She had snuck into the room behind me. 'Doesn't go to school.

Runs all around town, playing, posing for pictures and taking chocolates as bribes.'

'Will be a great model one day, Thaatha. She didn't remember me at the station.' I made a camera symbol with both my hands, clicking my tongue, as the imp posed.

'Come to Madras and act in movies,' I said.

'Take her, Yamuna,' said Saradamma, her mother. It was the tone of a mother who was proud of her precocious daughter. Mallika stuck her tongue out and scooted off.

Thaatha and I sat down on the floor, near the courtyard, for dinner. I ate rice meant for at least three people and finished the meal off with beeda. I didn't actually like betel leaves, but when Thaatha asked if I wanted one, I felt important. As if I'd been let into some old boys' club. He'd never asked before.

After dinner, he sank into his planter's chair and napped for a while. It was his pre-sleep nap. I went upstairs to my mother's room. My parents had spent the weekend here. My mother's sarees were still hung out to dry on the coat stand. I'd missed them by a few hours, Saradamma said. I hadn't called them. Or picked up when they called. They had this knack for figuring out what was going on with me by the exact length of my 'fines' and 'okays' over the phone. I decided that it was best to talk to them after I resolved my man-friend and property issues. Had she thwarted me before I had a chance to make my case to Thaatha? Wily Amma.

The old bed creaked when I sat on it. The ceiling fan was noisy. I fell in and out of sleep, dreaming of open fields and sunsets, garbage and cobwebs, of cockroaches in my food and lizards watching me menacingly from the ceiling.

Then I dreamt I was falling. I woke up with a jolt and realised I was no longer on the train. It was 7 a.m.

I went downstairs, laptop in hand. Coffee, hot, was waiting.

'I don't think I've had such good coffee even in Madras recently. You'll teach me the proportions?' I asked Saradamma.

I decided to buy beans from the Chettiar kadai down the road before going back home. Make my own coffee powder like her. Decoction from fresh ground peaberry, some chicory, fresh boiled milk and sugar. As Saradamma broke down the secret to her perfect drug—which convinced me that one needed a full-time cook around to have a decent cup of coffee—I felt my headache thaw into a pleasant fog. There was something absolutely comforting about not having to make my own coffee in the morning. It made me feel like a brat, a well-cared-for one. There's no way to drink a decent cup of filter coffee without burning your hands; everything scalding hot; the filter, the davara, the tumbler. And it's easier to make a bad cup of filter coffee than a good one.

'Where did we stop last?' Thaatha asked, looking down at me, through his glasses. He knew I'd be back with more questions. And he seemed ready. He had some old books in hand, and had circled paragraphs in a few of them, made dog ears in others. His coffee tumbler sat precariously on one arm of the Bombay fornicator. With his glasses and a head full of thick white hair, he looked much like an old professor. Respectable, with an air of confidence, but weary of life. Once, when an aunt had said that every day after one turned seventy was a bonus, he'd interjected,

'Punishment. Not bonus.' He'd waited for death, patiently, every day since he'd lost his wife. Each night he went to sleep smiling, saying, 'Hopefully, this will be it.' A morbid goodnight.

I was beginning to tire of my PhD, and was even considering giving it up altogether. What I wanted was gossip, family gossip to be precise, about my grandaunt and her wedding. And my grandfather's love story. But I had to pretend to care about work before I could work my way into asking him about all that. Most of our conversations started off with work, but were almost always about family. He knew it too, but pretended otherwise.

I was researching early twentieth-century music in Tamil Nadu when I had this idea of exploring it through memoirs and other personal writings of artistes. Because Thaatha worked in the Tamil and Telugu cinema industries, he was intimate with many dancers and singers. I chose to work on this because of him, of how he spoke about the music of his youth. I grew up hearing about musicians and their inner lives. He was very cosmopolitan in the way he understood women, especially women artistes.

Of course, the other reason I was drawn to this topic was my grandaunt, Lalitha. I wondered if I should ask Thaatha about the letter I'd found. But I couldn't bring myself to ask him about it just then. To tell him that I had read something so intimate. I caught myself thinking I'd only have to wait a little longer to get my hands on more, if he had them. No! I would rather my grandfather lived, with all his mystery intact, than die, leaving me to inherit his letters. What was it about this city that made death seem so close?

'You were getting ready to go to a Tamil Isai Sangam concert,' I prompted him.

'Ah … yes … Some people still say, what's a Carnatic concert without a Telugu song? But I attended the Tamil Isai Sangam concerts every year. It was first in Gokhale Hall on Armenian Street, then Raja Annamalai Chettiar Hall, and every time I attended a concert I was surprised by the amount of research performers put in to find those old Tamil compositions. Those were days of such unrest.'

'I should have been around then in the Forties in Madras. There was revolution in the air everywhere. So much happening, so much excitement, kadha?'

'No revolution is without collateral damage,' he said, stroking his chin.

He often made these mysterious statements and offered no explanation. Over the next hour, Thaatha talked about people from his past. I couldn't remember things from months ago. There he was, detailing things that had happened forever ago. About the many December music season venues in Madras, performers and the songs they performed on specific dates. He referred to the notes in his library every now and then, but mostly recalled things from memory.

A little later, I found myself battling another headache; I might have to inhale Karvol to clear the sinus out. Saradamma brought us another strong coffee, and Thaatha and I decided to continue later.

'I told you not to wash your hair,' she scolded me. 'At least unknot your hair and let it dry properly.'

'All mothers are the same,' Thaatha said.

Which reminded me of mine. And my house. I couldn't find a way to bring that up either. So I muttered to Thaatha, 'I found this letter,' and handed it over to him. A brief smile, and then what seemed like worry passed through his eyes.

'I'd like to read some more of these if you have?' I asked tentatively.

'You read this? Why?' He was surprisingly curt. Angry even.

'Ummm ...'

'You must not seek things that you neither have claim over nor have been given custody of. This is not yours to inherit,' he said, all formal, as if he were a lawyer reading a will, and left in a huff.

Did he yell at me over a harmless old letter, or did he know why I was here? I was pretty sure then that my mother must have received the power of attorney she'd been asking for, because I hadn't brought up anything about an inheritance with him. Perhaps I had lost already.

I withdrew to the bedroom and darkened it fully with Saradamma's help. I stuffed sarees and bedsheets in all the gaps so no light would come in, and switched on the fan. I tied a dupatta around my temple like I was off to war. And in the silence, I fought my sinus to sleep. My head was a molten mess. Heavy. My nose burnt. I managed to sleep for four hours. When I woke up, no one was around. I put on my shoes and decided to walk around town a bit.

# 3

# The Dead and the Deities

Hanuman Ghat was just as I remembered it. Some boys were chanting in a sing-song drawl. The smell of cow dung fused with that of vibhuti on the streets. The air was thick and stood still, the way it did in homes inhabited only by the old. A painting of Hanuman carrying the Sanjeevi hill; a big fat mouse feasting on a bowl of laddoos; a tiger chasing a deer like an Eighties movie villain; wrestlers training for a kushti match. A group of men carried a dead body, chanting 'Ram naam satya hai', with a trumpet and a dholak leading the procession. Buffaloes jostled for space with rickshaws, and men wrapped in heavily embroidered silk shawls and dhotis made their way swiftly to the ghat. Sarees hung in chaotic grace from balconies; telephone and broadband wires twisted around each other until you couldn't tell which was which, criss-crossing from lamp post to homes across the streets. Bikes and cycles leant against walls, and dogs and cats seemed untroubled by the hustle and bustle. As I walked, taking photos on my phone, I almost forgot where I was going.

When I felt that extra nip in the air, I put my phone away and looked up.

The first time I was here, I had walked all the way down the steps of the ghats, where it seemed like the clothes of the entire city were being washed and dried. I crossed men lathered up fully, children oiled up for a big bath, women baring their bosoms, uninhibited, and waded into the water.

I'd been disgusted by the very idea of a bath there. The water was murky green, dirty beyond comprehension. But my grandfather absolutely insisted I take a dip.

I held my nose and went in. Flowers floated about as did dark-coloured filth. Even the flowers had death written on them. I stepped in, with my clothes on, all the way down and immersed myself fully. And for a second, just one tiny second as I came out, I felt light.

'You've rid yourself of all your sins now. You are so lucky to have come here so young,' Thaatha said. If I were to count the ways I've sinned since, I'd have to live in Banaras and float on the Ganga for the rest of my life. This is why people come to Kashi after they're done with life, in their final years. When they're ready to embrace death, to wash away their sins.

I sat on the banks and watched the placid river playing host to the sins of the dead and their kin. A group of men dressed in new white dhotis sat next to their wives and performed some ritual. I wondered where my ashes would go. Possibly Madras's beaches. That was a small source of comfort. That I'd be a part of eternity in the sands of my beautiful Marina. Or the Besant Nagar beach. It was a bit too yuppie, but that's where the electric crematorium was. Maybe I should donate my body to a medical hospital?

As I mentally wrote a will giving my body away to science and then to the beaches of Madras, by turns,

Nataraj, Thaatha's regular boatman showed up on the ghats. I asked him if he would take me on a ride.

The November evening mist took over as seagulls chased boats. People settled along the stairs to the ghat after hunting for the perfect spot to witness the arti from. Even after the arti, I was not in the mood to go home. I wandered around the narrow gullies and found myself at the Vishwanath temple. I walked into the temple aimlessly and left soon after. I didn't pray. I never did. The literal only thing expected of women, said a master who came to my best friend's house to teach her scriptural wisdom on Thursdays, was to be a pathivratha. We were thirteen and giggling. He said, no need to even pray, just work for your husband, bear him children, be true to him, that will get you the highest place in heaven.

Thanks, no thanks, sir.

But going in to the Vishwanath temple made me feel like I'd have a good answer for when people asked me what I did in Banaras. I ate kulfi after the temple visit. Slowly, the numbing of senses that comes from a change of landscape subsided, and I extricated myself from the chaos of the streets to think. I realised I wasn't wearing shoes. They'd been forgotten at the temple. I walked back, eating another kulfi, to find my shoes.

A brown-white pregnant cow had decided to settle in for the night right in front of Thaatha's house. As I jumped in, trying to avoid its tail, I almost hit my head against the wooden panel of dancing apsaras on the wall. Thaatha, who had been waiting near the door, took my hand.

'I have been anticipating this. That's why I decided to wait here,' he said, smiling; vibhuti back on his forehead.

He must have felt bad about yelling at me for reading the letter.

'Don't stay out very late, kannu. I am not sure it's safe,' Saradamma said. That vague threat. It sounded harmless enough, her worry, but I watched her daughter play inside the house and knew she feared for Mallika as well. That threat of physical harm was like an evil spirit that has followed me everywhere I've gone for as long as I can remember.

Growing up, the bus had been the very embodiment of this threat for me. The romance and fun of the bus that I saw in Mani Ratnam movies remained out of my grasp. When I first felt that threat chill my bones, imprint itself on my veins and very being, I was in class eight. I was on my way back home from school, dressed in grey knee-length pinafore, hair in two tight braids, tied up with white ribbons. I was just beginning to understand fashion. I'd learnt to fold my socks down, and not wear it all the way up like a nerd. I took a teeny bit of hair from my braid and let it hang loose in front of my face. My mother hated it. I was carrying a really cool denim backpack and a jute water bottle bag.

I could see that day any time I wanted in my mind's eye, as if I were having an out-of-body experience. Feel how I felt and remember the wind and the 'sudden brakes' pushing me around, ever-so-lightly, like a drunk, inside the bus. What the outside looked like, what the air inside smelled like.

It was the day I learnt to make my ordinary ribbons posh. Instead of stitching the ends of the white ribbon, I'd learnt from the hippest girl in class to poke holes on the edges of the ribbon with a lit agarbatti and cut the holes in half. It looked pretty damn good. I was proud. In the bus, I was feeling the edges of my ribbon, looking out the window, standing near the entrance, holding the bar in front of me for support. A man tapped me and passed change to buy ticket. I turned to pass the money along, then realised that the conductor was not near me. He was, in fact, on the other side of the bus, closer to the man who'd tapped me. I looked back at the man in confusion, when I felt something wet in my left hand. The man, who must have been in his twenties, looked me in the eye and then looked down. I followed his gaze. His penis was hanging out. Right there in the not-full evening bus. But it seemed no one else was seeing what I was seeing. There were three little girls in front of him. All I thought of then was, 'I hope they don't turn around.' I threw the change down and looked away, confused, shocked, disgusted all at once. He held a long notebook to cover himself every time the bus stopped.

That was just the first time. There were several others. Men pushing their erect penises against me while the bus was full, jam-packed and there was nowhere to go. Of hands that grazed, eyes that undressed, breasts that were pinched and hips held against will. All before I'd even turned fifteen.

When I returned to the gentle fold of the old house from images of buses from so long ago that they seemed like they'd happened to someone else, the guest rooms were open. More people had come. Thaatha rented out some rooms to people doing the oblation circuit. Allahabad, Banaras and Gaya, to pray for the departed in their lives.

For Thaatha, though, this city was not part of that circuit. It was his last stop. Before salvation, he said. He wanted to be cremated in Manikarnika Ghat. To be led by Shiva to the other world, he said. That's why he moved to his home in Banaras. This is where he cremated my grandmother, after which he turned into an utterly and unrecognisably devout man. He had put every ounce of energy left in his body into reaching this town. One that the boatman Nataraj called the big masaan, the great graveyard.

I asked Thaatha why he turned to belief. And why so late.

'I have to hope that it doesn't end here. How can it be that your grandmother and I are done? How can I be alive like this when she isn't? I feel small knowing how little control I have over this life. I had to surrender, because the choice was between faith and despair. I chose to believe that even though I can no longer see her, I can feel her. I can have conversations with her. The dead and the deities play the same role in the lives of the living. They are who we must turn to with life's questions.'

I didn't know how to respond.

'Is everything okay at home?'

He wasn't happy about my live-in situation, but he was not the sort to interfere, and he knew me well enough to realise that I had been upset and preoccupied since I arrived.

I said, 'Hmmm. I am not so sure.'

'Hmmm,' he said, not knowing what else to say either.

I stood against one of the pillars near the courtyard and looked around at the house. People had come and gone, but the house, over a hundred years old, had remained. Like the town it was in. I walked to the courtyard and scratched the stalk of the tulasi plant to see if it was alive. It wasn't. I slowly extricated it from the pot, looking at the people staring down from the photos, at me. My great grandmother, grandmother, her brothers.

My mother had these framed and hung some years ago, so Thaatha would have some familiar faces to look at. And then I saw her. My grandaunt. Lalitha.

# 4

# A Songstress and an Anomaly

My grandaunt Lalitha, who'd joked about her husband looking like Hitler, who'd been married away at fourteen, grew up to be an icon of sorts. In all her photographs, she was a picture of frenzy, hands up in the air, in motion, forehead crinkled, eyes shut, mouth open. Sitting a little away from the microphone, always. She didn't trust it.

Almost every news article on her spoke about Lalitha's onstage personality. That's what brought her a cult following. If you heard her, if you were her student, if you learnt a song or two from her, if you accompanied her, if you had a recording of hers, it was understood that you were not the typical Carnatic music audience or performer. Especially in the Sixties and Seventies. Her concerts were seldom sold out—she was what they called a 'performer's performer'. Other artistes showed up to listen every time she sang.

'I mean, she was a lot of fun offstage too. Can you imagine, such a senior classical artiste, a legend, running around, playing with her grown-up students on the beach? She would feed all of us ice creams on some days, and send us home without teaching us a single note. She was fun like that. She didn't treat music class like it was punishment. And onstage, that was magnified a hundred times. Her sense of style, grace, flamboyance … she was something else. And she was riveting to watch. I think she single-handedly made Gold Spot popular among the Carnatic audience. She used to sip it in the middle of her concert. Everyone else drank sukku coffee, tea, kashayam. Amma drank only Gold Spot.' That's about all I managed to get from Arundhati Raman, one of Lalitha's best-known students. She spoke more about herself than Lalitha for the better part of three hours. 'She heard me sing one day and immediately told my father, she's going to become very big. You send her to me from tomorrow, and encouraged me.' I'd met a string of artistes a year or so ago, interviewing them about her.

Lalitha's concert sarees were always simple but her blouses always had a zari border. She never hid her blouse as other women singers did, wrapping the free end of the saree around their shoulders.

'A brooch held the saree in place, and she never suffered a wardrobe malfunction,' my mother said to me once. It apparently happened to a friend of Lalitha's. That young singer had been scarred by it when she was just seventeen or eighteen, and gave up the stage altogether. Her saree moved a bit, and a murmur moved through the crowd. Oso—one side only, meaning one of her breasts was seen. You could see nothing, it was just the blouse that you saw, and it was as if the very shape of it titillated and scandalised everyone, even the women.

Lalitha famously collected brooches, and she had so many of them. It became something of a fashion statement.

She was herself something of a fashion icon. People came to her concert as much to listen to her main ragam as they did for the brooch and the blouse. Fans would send her brooches from across the world, studded with pearls, even precious stones. She wore her pottu closer to her eyebrows, and not in the middle of her forehead, and usually it was vadamalli, magenta. Not maroon or red.

She was accompanied by women almost exclusively whenever she played in Madras. Rukmani on mridangam and Soundaravalli on violin. They were a famous trio—a novelty that won them many concerts in the early years.

Kumari Nair, who played the violin for all of Lalitha's Kerala concerts, came down to Madras and attended her remembrance day some years ago. 'Lalitha's rapport with her peers was enviable, on and off the stage,' she had said. 'She would be in the middle of a note, and just with her hands and eyes she would make a very simple gesture, as if she were turning a page or dimming a kerosene oil lamp, and the mridangist and I would know immediately that a slower bit was coming up. She cared about us, even while she was immersed in her music. It's not necessary, but it's the courteous thing to do, and you could always count on Lalitha to follow that dharma. It's what those who respect their accompanists do. She arrived early to every single concert, and because she sat so far away from the mic, she ensured no sound was out of place, and everyone's output was the same volume. Her concerts were iconic because she paid attention to these things that others took for granted. I could come in at the last minute, knowing full well I was in good hands. The soundcheck was done by a perfectionist, after all.'

In nearly every interview she gave, Lalitha spoke of her mistrust of the microphone. She felt it didn't throw her voice the way she intended it to.

'My job as a musician is the search for my own pure voice. It's a pity that the only time I can hear it is in the confines of my own home, when I am alone, practising,' she rued. 'What it does is make my own voice a stranger to me. And this truly comes in the way of how I perceive what I am singing. I am doing everything by approximation and guesswork up there. It's not clean. It feels like I'm cheating.'

Lalitha attended several micless sessions in the homes of women artistes across the city in her late teens. Tondiarpet, George Town, Parrys Corner. These had a profound impact on her. She felt that her mind worked differently, processed music differently without the shackles of a microphone. She felt unencumbered without it. Lalitha credited her close confidante and actor Hamsammal for not only reviving her career but also teaching her to embrace music in this wholly different manner. As a practice, as a way of making sense of life.

In an interview in the late 1940s, Lalitha spoke about how she came to learn music from her friend:

> At one private terrace concert I did something I am not proud of. I performed a song no one taught me. Hamsammal was in the audience. She stormed out of the house. I was very flustered, but I finished the song somehow. A few days later, agonised by the image of Hamsammal leaving, I asked a friend to take me to her. She was so hospitable when I went to see her.
>
> 'A song from a school must be taught by a guru to her student, don't you think?' she asked, her voice calm. Not betraying any anger.

'I heard you sing it and fell in love with it. Then I heard it on the radio. And then again and again at concerts. I was greedy to make it my own. I apologise if I have crossed a line,' I said.

'It is a beautiful song, there's no doubt.' Hamsammal smiled. 'Anybody can sing anything they want to. But to perform it onstage, don't you think there must be a trail?' Her tone was searching. 'If hearing it is enough to perform, why does anyone need a guru anymore? Songs come from schools, schools have a bani, they carry the imprints of our gurus and their legacies. Can legacies be sullied like this?'

I had no answer. So she showed me the way out. My heart was heavy for days afterwards, I couldn't sing at all. Every time I tried to sing, I felt like a thief harvesting stolen land. I went again to her home, uninvited, on Vijayadasami, determined to right my wrong. I bought flowers, fruits, tambulam, borrowed some money from my sister and then I surrendered. That's how she became my guru and my saviour, and later, my best friend. I needed her, and she barely needed to notice me. That she did and gave me the invaluable gift of her mentorship made me feel visible again. I sensed myself changing. Hamsammal's tutelage at once gave me courage and hope. The despair of a hidden life lifted ever so slowly. She taught me to stay with my art. To not want to stray with it … take it here and there. As if I were an impatient child whose music was enslaved to recognition. To not just expect from art but to give my *self* up to it. To pour my self into the art. To nurture the music in me and to treat it with dignity. She was able to identify a voice that I had long lost to life. Is this any small gift?

Sometime in the late 1940s Lalitha was interviewed by *Life* magazine, along with her starlet-singer, mentor-friend Hamsammal. I chanced upon it in a blog that archived vintage women-in-sarees photos. Lalitha wore an embroidered blouse with delicate lacework running along the collar and sleeves and a thick cotton saree, and Hamsammal wore a bewitchingly gorgeous silk saree fit for a queen. They were sitting across each other, tamburas on the floor of a terrace, their hair and laughter free, looking like they were up to no good, evoking joy and enviable camaraderie. The thrill of seeing Lalitha in a blog I loved had added in no small measure to my feverish need to know her more. Underneath their photos, there was a quote each from the women—one from a long lineage of women performers, and the other, a first-generation performer. I wondered if it was a conversation the two had that evening during the photoshoot.

Lalitha: All of us, women artistes of my generation, are being forced to find answers to questions thrust on us. What does dignity mean to us? Being a family woman, or being able to pursue art?

Hamsammal answered with her own two brilliant questions: Why can't any woman decide for herself what she wants to be? Isn't there space for all of us to do what we want to do in this new, independent India?

When I called C.V. Vittal, a cantankerous twenty-something star singer who'd called Lalitha his musical inspiration in a Facebook post, he instantly agreed to speak. We met at a bar for lunch. I had heard him sing just once on YouTube, but he didn't care if I had. He didn't seem to care that I was related to Lalitha either. He'd psychoanalysed her every move and was happy to present his theories to anyone who cared to listen.

'You know, the way she defied everyone and wore her saree like that in public, like a starlet, from a young age …' he said between sips of his drink. 'She must have loved the stage, the feeling of being up there. I love it, so I can relate to this. I pick my clothes with great attention too. She was uninhibited. That's what made her music what it was. If you see her pictures, she is so carefree. She doesn't care if her hand, missing finger and all, is on camera. She doesn't care about what profile the photo is taken from. Trust me, I learn from a senior lady artiste, and they care a lot about that shit. She doesn't even care if she looks bad in a picture. That's what makes her so badass. Art is not all grace and poise. It's also hurt and ego and megalomania and self-respect.'

When I brought up the whole audience thing, he didn't quite see it the way I did. He saw a larger conspiracy. 'Who or what has a cult following? Those rejected by the mainstream, right? The "regular audience", they never took to her, why? It's all symptomatic of a deeper malaise. There were murmurs of some scandal, but no one knows the details much anymore. You should look into that. I mean, my theory is that that's why they never accepted her.'

'What scandal?' I'd asked. I was clueless. Utterly.

He stopped eating. 'I don't know. You're like her grandniece. You should know?'

'I don't know. I mean—'

He'd shrugged and asked for another whisky sour. 'There's something there, I guess.'

# 5
# Rejection

The next day, I shopped at my favourite store. I needed a break from thinking about those bloody letters and that bloody house. Thaatha called his regular rickshawala.

'I could get used to these comforts,' I said.

'No? I love it here too. Gopal, you take her around and then come home for lunch,' he winked.

They'll do a beeda session without me today. I'd borrowed Thaatha's shawl. I'd spent some time in front of the mirror and was feeling good about myself. My hair was behaving. My short wraparound skirt was a bit of a tease and my tee-shirt sat snug. It was cold but you don't fight the instinct that tells you what to wear when you want to look good. Cycle bells, buses, autorickshaws, the crowds on the roads, the chaotic medley as my rickshaw rattled slowly down the road towards the ghat put me in a better mood. The honking kept me firmly anchored in the present. Who needs mindfulness apps on these streets?

'My children are asking for a mobile phone. What is a good model? With camera?' Gopal asked me when he heard me taking photos from my phone.

'You have children?'

'Haan. Teen,' he said and showed me a photo of him, wife and three kids.

'How old are you?' I asked and then felt stupid for asking him that.

'Twenty-three,' he said.

I smiled at him and he flashed a quick smile before turning back. His teeth were perfectly aligned. Gave me a complex instantly.

'I am not sure. But I will ask around and call you before I leave, okay?'

'Sure,' he said. 'My children and wife are back in Bihar. I go back only when there is rain, to work on my land. Otherwise I am here, with the rickshaw.' Shehnai strains, rhythm pads and a too-sweet-to-be-true Alka Yagnik sang *Ghoonghat ki aad se dilbar ka* from the small music player attached to the handlebar.

At the store, Nikhil's face lit up as soon as he saw me. We sat sipping chai, making eyes and whispering uncomfortably, sitting on terribly uncomfortable stools as the other boys in the shop, his brothers, flitted about busily. Finally, he sent them away to the next room to do some rearranging.

'So what's new?' I asked, picking out some pants that were made from old Banarasi sarees.

'You would look amazing in this,' he said, throwing a blue shawl around me. He was a few inches shorter than I was. Had he gotten chubbier since I last saw him? He smelled amazing, as always. And there was something comforting about that deep voice. It was like a switch. An instant turn on.

'My mother would love this,' I said.

'Take it then. Don't pay for that one, pay for the others though.' He smiled a good-natured smile.

The last time I'd seen Nikhil, several months ago, he'd said he was open to the idea of 'us'.

'There was never an us,' I tried to reason.

'There was. Just because you don't acknowledge it …' he drifted off.

We hadn't spoken after that. I asked him to help wrap another shawl around me to see how it would look.

Nikhil and I met through a friend. When she found out I was going to be in Banaras, my college classmate Anandi sent him a text message introducing me. We met over coffee. He was about the same age as me and *not at all* interested in relationships. Nikhil was a walking cliché, an advertisement for the Orkut era; listed both Ayn Rand and Albert Camus as his favourite writers. He made for great travel company though, and I found it utterly original at that point that he didn't want a relationship. I thought that was a cool thing back in the 2000s. We hung out often through that summer. He was running his family shop after an MBA from the UK.

One night in hot and stuffy Banaras, after a few shots of vodka with pepper, we both loosened up more than we should have. He took me to a friend's place, kicking the friend out for the night. There was no hesitation. Or waiting. Or signals to read. All the flirting over drinks had made it clear to both of us that we were going to have sex.

Back in the room, we kissed hurriedly, as if our minds would change if we didn't. We undressed just as swiftly, without even drawing the curtains or switching off the light. I'd loved the certainty with which we were heading towards things. Vodka did its thing.

Afterwards, he said, I love you. It was unnecessary, contrived even. Like some trick. I thought about it for a second and decided I couldn't love him, I didn't know him at all. And I knew that this night would have been very different but for the alcohol. So I hugged him and almost as an afterthought said, 'I love you too.' It seemed like the polite thing to do. I figured that he said it because he just wanted to make the most of the moment or that he was very drunk. Or both. I didn't quite grasp then that you didn't need the promise of a future to feel what he felt. Or say what he did.

'Do you want to hang out tonight?' I asked Nikhil as I tried on the free copper sulphate shawl I'd winged for Amma from him. Casually, without seeming too eager. Then my eyes caught the light in his and I knew where this was headed already. I suddenly felt my throat close up.

'Want to catch a movie?' he asked, smiling. A bright, warm smile that broke my heart.

But I wasn't done being a bitch. I leant in, placed my lips as close to his ears as possible, almost brushing against them, and whispered so that the boys in the next room wouldn't accidentally hear me.

'Actually, I am alone, on the first floor in Thaatha's house.'

He stepped back and breathed out loud; his cheeks deflated, like balloons. It was a rebuff. Then I just stood there, waiting for him to say something. He did not. And I continued to just stand there, unable to move. Folding the shawl in my hands over and over again until it was all crumpled. The red-hot embarrassment of an in-person rejection feels like hot milk scorching the insides of your ears. The world is white, frothing in anger, and your ears burn.

Finally he said, 'I don't think so.'

I felt my face burning but couldn't say anything.

In the wee hours of the morning, I woke up and texted Sundar.

'Let's end this.'

I knew then in my heart that it was finally, really over. I was even calm. I'd passed the hurt on. At first, he didn't respond. And when he did, it was such meaningless banter that we both knew it was over. I asked him to leave the key with the neighbour's watchman, Kumar-anna.

And that was it, one minute I was in a relationship, the next I wasn't. I didn't know if it was the place, spending time with Thaatha, or if it was the humiliation of the previous day. I had found the courage to leave.

That day, I stayed home, mostly reading. I didn't go for the arti either. Thaatha did.

I woke up from a nap to a rude thumping. The urgency of whoever it was at the door was beginning to worry me as I ran down the stairs, hoping it wouldn't be a health emergency of some sort. When you live with the old, every alarm—the phone, the doorbell, a loud thud in the next room—appears ominous. I chided myself; it must just be courier or water can or some inane delivery service. It was Mallika, who couldn't reach the door handle.

# 6
# Chengalpattu

Back in Chengalpattu, I realised that a wasp had laid the foundations for its home on my kitchen window. At first it was fascinating to see its goings and comings, the wasp building a safe space right under my nose. As I watched from the other side of the glass, its home grew in size. And then a sort of disgust and fear crept up on me. I wanted the gross shit-coloured nest off my window. But I was scared to do anything because I didn't want to be stung. So I watched. Paralysed as it happily mooched off of my carefully built home. A home that I wanted to make my own, but how was I ever going to? I'd chickened out of even mentioning my fight with Amma over the house to Thaatha.

With a knife, I tapped rudely on the glass from the inside. When the wasp left, I thought I'd won my home back. But later, when I was slicing butter and throwing it into a pan, I noticed its return. I lit a match and tried to heat the glass from the inside. It felt cruel but I had no choice. Anyway, it had no effect on the wasp. I switched on the torch light on my phone and moved it from one side to another. It followed the light like a drunk for a while and then ignored me. That's how I came to live with a wasp when Sundar was gone. All his things gone. There was a Sundar-sized hole in every square foot of the house. I closed my eyes and wondered if he had ever choked his ex-wife, like he did to me in the middle of an argument before I left for Banaras. I ran the question over and over again in my head.

I made tea with lots of ginger and sat in the balcony. I wondered what the view was like when my grandmother sat there. All I saw were apartment buildings in various stages of construction across the road, and bikes going up and down the road, with fathers and sons carrying out their duties. Grocery shopping; dropping daughters, wives and sisters to work, college, schools; ferrying water. I lit a lamp in the alcove in my balcony, and sure enough the winged termites came.

We were always in the company of winged visitors, growing up too. If you didn't shut every single crack of your home at 6 p.m. sharp, you could forget about peace of mind that night. It started with swarms of mosquitoes over your oily head, moving when you moved, like a halo in those mythological films in Eastmancolor. Then they attached themselves to any dark surface or space in the house. Especially the many travel bags given as gifts at the functions my parents attended throughout the year.

When you switched off the lights to sleep, or watch TV, they would come as an army, sucking the very life out of you, the pinpricks across your face, arms and legs impossible to ignore. At dusk, we'd shut all the doors of the house, and one of us, usually this was me, took mosquito repellent mats, those soft fragrant blue flat ones that looked like a memory chip, and held them on tongs over the stove. They'd catch fire right away. I would turn the fire off after I was convinced they had burnt enough, and go room by room with the smoky Good Knight mats, leaving them in and shutting the door. Even then, I suspected, the mosquitoes merely fainted and didn't actually die. If you took your ears close to the floor, you could hear the low hum of the insects. After fifteen minutes, I'd go back to each room and sweep the mosquitoes up in a plastic tray and throw them out. About a few hundred of them from each room. And then, when those mosquito-killer bats made their way to Burma Bazaar, we bought two, as if we were going to play badminton. We took turns electrocuting mosquitoes by the dozens, and revelling in the scent of their burnt corpses. Sometimes, I woke up in the middle of the night to my mother standing by my head, sweeping the air with the bat. Pat. Pat. Pat. Pat. Pat. Zzzz. Mosquitoes would sometimes burn, die and fall on my face. I'd wipe them off and go back to sleep, smiling. This too was love, I'd think.

And then there were those crickets. Sevuthu kozhi. They came in through the bathroom drain, I think, and lodged themselves under one of our beds or underneath the spare gas cylinder that was kept by the toilet attached to my room. In the darkness and silence of our tiny rooms, the call of the crickets (sometimes there was more than one) echoed, amplified by the hollow suitcases or cylinders under which they hid. It is impossible to even sit about, forget sleep, while a cricket croaks itself hoarse right under your head.

My brother would come to my room as soon as he heard it, broom and chappals in one hand and torchlight in the other, dressed in his banian and shorts. He would squat under my bed like a predator. And wait patiently, turning the torch on and off. On and off. We wouldn't say a word to each other, we didn't want the cricket to know we were around. This would go on for an hour or so sometimes. I would be reading a book or listening to the Walkman, or just lying there with my eyes open and staring at the ceiling. He would just squat there on the floor in what we called 2B (two bathroom) position.

Some days he was triumphant. He'd manage to catch the cricket in motion. He would slam his chappal hard against the insect. Splat! And it would lie there. Silent, slippery, its white-brown mucousy innards spilt. We never felt bad for it. Always only triumphant joy. Our parents seemed to mind neither the noise nor our murderous proclivities. They pretended to not even notice any of this. Or perhaps they didn't. On most days though, the crickets got the better of my brother.

'Ada thu!' he'd spit as he slammed his own door shut.

We also had flying cockroaches in the bathroom that explored other parts of the home, emboldened by the darkness of the night. If you slept on the floor on a plastic or straw mattress—like we all did at some point in that house, before beds became a thing—you were sure to have woken up to a cockroach on your legs or face, even under your clothes.

Once, an older uncle staying with us, who wasn't as unsentimental as my parents, spotted two lizards running across my body as I lay asleep. He immediately referenced the Gowli Panchangam and declared that I would live very long. He'd sometimes talk to the lizards when they made their tut-tut noises in the house. Or claim to have received a divine answer to a question he'd been mulling over.

Just a week before my uncle declared that I'd live long, a lizard had fallen on my head while I was bathing. Crashing down from the ceiling to land on my hair. I shrieked and shrieked. And the same uncle had mortified me by saying that I must be careful. Lizard on your head meant sudden death. I figured the two cancelled each other out and resorted to sleeping with the bedsheet covering me entirely, even my head. I made sure not an inch of my body was exposed to the creatures. And yet they've always found me. One afternoon, as I napped, something huge jumped through the window and on to me. My heart froze, not knowing what had fallen and I pushed whatever it was hard. It flew through the room, making a meowww sound.

And then there were the centipedes. Amma said they were called 'jerry' in Telugu, and that sounded cute. But those fast creepy crawlies seemed to always upset her. An aunt told her that it was because I was mingling with everyone and touching everything while on my period, and that they only came during my period.

Kailasanathar Street had changed from the time my grandmother lived here. But the winged termites had stayed. The old, large, charmingly impractical homes had all been broken down, and in their place were cramped but efficient apartment buildings. The road had been widened and the bathrooms moved inside homes. Even in my childhood, they were outside the home. The drains on the sides of the roads did not keep up with the twenty-first century plumbing though. Sewage stench from the road reached my balcony. I tried to resist with a lavender diffuser.

The ginger from the tea went coursing through my body. I felt as if, at last, things were as they should be. *Ab ke sawan ghar aaja*, Begum Akhtar commanded with that voice of hers that was all love and sorcery. I felt my nerves unknot. That feeling of panic, like I was drowning, like if I didn't fix things my life would end, that desperation slowly began to fade.

The rest of the day, I vegetated on the sofa. Asahi and Djarums for company.

I'd 'borrowed' some old letters and photos that were in a file in my grandfather's room before sneaking out of Banaras, and sifted through unfamiliar faces, notes and letters, wedding invitations smeared in turmeric and death announcement cards, their edges blackened to declare mourning.

Most of it was happily mundane. In Ellis Dungan's *Ambikapathy*, Thyagaraja Bhagavathar played the male lead. My very young grandfather also played a small cameo. He had to attach a wig and a large beard. Was offered Rs 50 as payment. I tried and failed to find him in a YouTube upload of the movie. Still, it was nice to know that, somewhere in that video, he was there. Immortalised. Whenever I missed him, I turned to YouTube, to find the songs he played the harmonium for. I pictured him, young, smiling, calm, part of the orchestra, handsome, suited up, in tortoise-shell wayfarers. His hands moving of their own will, like he was only breathing, not making music.

On my speaker, *Pani … Pani Bhare Re Kaun* … sang Badi Moti Bai, the words delivered with perfect crispness.

Her voice was sweet, just not sickly sweet like that of playback singers. It was the voice of confidence. She meandered playfully here and there. It was like playing a game of hide-and-seek by a gentle stream.

I wondered if my grandaunt, who must have been singing around the same time as her, sang like that too as a young woman. Her mouth wide open, from deep inside.

In some time, though, I was staring at the store room, hungry. No cup noodles, no eggs, no idli batter. The house was quiet, except for the crickets outside.

The doorbell finally saved me from the misery of the empty store room.

# 7

# A Surprise

I ran back into the bedroom, hid the letters in my cupboard, shoving it into the mess of all the new pants I'd bought from Nikhil. I'd been trying to prove a point by spending all that money in his shop, but I couldn't remember what it was. I looked through the magic eye again. And scooted off to throw the beer cans away. I washed my face and sprayed the room with my deodorant before going back to the door.

'Thaatha, how did you get here?'

'I took a flight to Delhi and from there to Madras,' he said. He sounded tired, but gave me the explanations I needed. 'Sarada booked the flight and I requested a wheelchair service. They put me in a cab too. You took off so suddenly, I was worried.' He looked about the house, almost tiptoeing around, as if he were gauging the situation and wondering whether he should stay or leave.

'No one's here. I am alone.'

'Oh.'

'So, you can now use your contacts to find me a suitably handsome, tall boy.'

'Is that all? No more conditions?'

'Preferably ultra-rich. Like rich rich. Not upper middle class and all.'

'Let me write this down, wait,' he said.

'Why can't I be rich? Like inherit-a-bungalow-and-a-car-and-a-factory rich?' I asked, bringing his suitcase in.

'Because your grandfather was a communist and your great grandfathers gambled every penny that came their way.'

I groaned.

He got straight to the point. 'I know you took my file.'

I looked away. How had he figured it out, he had a million files!

'I am sorry. I didn't think you'd mind.'

'I did mind,' he said flatly.

'You are staying a while, right?' I asked.

I carried more of his luggage into the guest room, running in to hide my embarrassment.

'Of course,' his voice softened a bit. 'There will be a reunion of some of my musician friends here in a few days.'

'I am so glad you are here,' I said, giving his hand a squeeze.

We had a quiet, early dinner and then he went off to sleep. I woke up the next morning to the incessant, happy chirping of sparrows near my balcony. And devotional music. We ate dosa and chutney.

Thaatha was listening to *Ellam Yesuve*. A black-and-white photo of Jikki, wearing a big pottu and flowers, smiled back from the smart TV.

'It might be the greatest devotional song written in India. I played the harmonium,' he smiled. 'This is also your mother's favourite song. I'd taught all of them, your mother, Lalitha, Subbu, to play this song on the harmonium. It made devotion seem not like something out of our grasp, not like something serious, not like something strenuous. It still brings a smile to my face when I hear the orchestra.'

'You're lucky you didn't have Twitter then to lynch you for becoming traitors to Hinduism and singing in praise of Christ.'

'Ayyayyo,' he hit his forehead, 'I read about it in the papers. There are so many albums sung by Hindus in praise of other gods and vice versa, what are they going to do, go back in time and boycott the dead? P.B. Srinivas's Christian songs were a genre unto themselves, you know? We did that one album, *Kelungal Tharapadum*, I think, with L.R. Easwari.'

When I left home after breakfast, SPB was earnestly singing a qawwali on Christ. *Karthar en maipar*.

I bought myself a paper cone full of hot roasted peanuts from the woman who boarded the suburban train behind me and found my spot. The last corner window seat. Legs folded up on the seat, I looked out the window as the city passed me by, quietly.

I had a book for the commute. My neighbour Rani recommended *Ladies Coupé* because I'd been on a train alone recently. A biscuit-coloured mutt, looking paavam, sat by my feet. A young wife with at least two muzhams of flowers wrapped around her head sat in front of me. Two older government-employee-type aunties called each other 'Maydaum', and exchanged office gossip. Up ahead, a young woman sold rosaries and beaded jewellery. I drifted off to the book.

My parents' home in Madras had the same green doors and windows as the Banaras home. We didn't have a compound wall or an entryway though. The house just opened out on to the road. I'd hated bringing my friends home because of this. This and the fact that my parents rented our outer wall to a saree shop. Their advertisement screamed out at anyone passing by Naidu Street. It was embarrassing because sometimes they painted men's underwear and bras on our walls.

What I did love though was that the house had three sets of doors that opened out onto the road. When the street died for the night, we could open all the doors. And we did. It felt like we owned Naidu street then. When my father was in town, the four of us—my parents, my brother and I—sat in the living room drinking hot masala milk that my father bought from a small bhavan nearby.

I got off at the Central station and took the metro back home.

'You are alive. Okay, good to know,' Arun said. My brother was leaving for work.

'You owe me two thousand rupees, remember?' I said, mock-hitting him on the head.

'You owe me like a million rupees for babysitting your ass, teaching you how to ride a scooter and for letting you lose my cycle.'

'Hello, what is this not-picking-up-phone business you have started?' Amma asked as she made her way into the kitchen, her hair dripping wet, tied in a knot near her waist.

Handing me coffee, she asked, 'What is wrong?'

When I pretended not to hear her, she asked again. 'So, what is it?'

'Nothing,' I said. And before she could say anything else, 'I liked this guy and it's not going to work out. Happy?'

'Let it go,' she said, giving my hand a squeeze, not looking at me. She took in a deep breath and then stopped short of saying something. She was being surprisingly nice. I thought she'd warn me or something, about men and love, like those movie ammas. But this was more than she was comfortable saying.

'Wait for a few minutes and then we can have lunch,' Amma said.

I looked up at my grandmother's photo in the living room. She wasn't smiling; her eyes pierced through the image.

'She was in a lot of pain at this point. We had to beg her to let us take one picture. Finally she said okay to one,' Amma said. 'We dressed her up and forced her to come to the studio. I am so glad we did, or we would have had nothing left of her. This is the only thing I have that's hers …'

Was the photo all she had of her mother? Didn't she know about the letters? There must be more like the ones I'd found. Or was she acting, like Thaatha was? I wanted to tell her, ask her. But I wasn't sure why Thaatha never did. Why she never did. So I said nothing.

Nana came out of his room and shouted at me. 'Why don't you ever call us?'

'I have just been a little busy. Work is hectic and I am a little nervous. Did Thaatha call you guys?'

'Yes. How is he? Why didn't you bring him along, Yamuna?' Amma asked.

'Didn't think he would enjoy another long car journey now,' I said, rinsing the plate handed to me.

No sooner had the first morsel hit my mouth, she blurted out, 'I got the power of attorney to the house.' A smirk danced on her lips. This was the first time either of us had mentioned the house directly with the other. I'd only made my displeasure known to Arun or my dad before this. She wanted me to know she'd beat me to it. I didn't say anything, as usual, because what could I say?

As if my mother's power-of-attorney bomb was not enough, I would learn something else that would make my headache come pounding back with a vengeance that evening. I wanted to finish reading the letters before Thaatha took them back, he hadn't asked me about them again. So I got to them as soon as I returned home post-lunch.

Imagine an enigma like Lalitha. A singer. A Padma awardee no less. A fashion icon whose brooches made it to Pinterest. Whose music had fans across the world. Imagine stealing letters from your own grandfather in the hope of finding out more about her exciting life.

Now imagine, discovering this instead: she was married at fourteen to a drinking, gambling priest. A raging wife-beater.

௨

17.9.1941
Chingleput

Dear Subbu,

I am well and wish to hear the same from you.

Here Amma's health is fading. She lies on the bench all day. Her frame is shrinking too. She is no longer the tallest woman in town. But nothing serious, so do not worry.

These days, I have taken to walking alone to the hillock behind our house to watch the Kolavai eri from up there. I tell everyone at home I am going to the temple. The lake and the view from the hill help me calm down. From up there, I can see far below and far across town. The earth up there is the sort of red that fills your eyes even as it plays hide-and-seek. It's everywhere and nowhere; you catch a glimpse of it and then you don't. Because it's also green everywhere. The grass, trees, shrubs, tiny flowering plants are all just packed into every inch of land. When I walk through the wide-open hill, I don't have the courage to stroll. It feels like the earth will cave under my feet if I don't lift my leg really fast. I see my own footprints violating the grass carpet and I quickly move. One of these days, though, I wish that I would forget to lift my feet and the earth would swallow me whole.

When the sun shines bright, the shadows of all the trees—coconut, drumstick, frangipani, guavas and nagalinga—merge into each other and you can't tell which is which. There are ant hills, some almost black, some the colour of the earth, tall and short ... every few feet. Twilight from up there is a bit strange, Subbu, I confess. The grass around my feet rustles every now and then, and I wish it were a snake and then wish it wouldn't be one. I've never seen a snake up there though. Whenever there's a breeze, the trees bow and bend gracefully.

I walk back home in the shadows, guided by my own intuition and the sounds of cow bells. Late in the evening, when I come back, plastering my forehead with vibhuti and kungumam, the house is quiet, but not so much as to worry me. At twilight, our wild garden looks like a painting. Clouds scattered about the sky, and hundreds of stars quietly talking to each other in a language of winks I cannot quite grasp. I enjoy sitting by the well in the backyard in complete silence as the late evening turns into night. Time does not exist. Only the sky and I, and its changing colours. In the dark of the night, sitting under the greys of the heavens, I am very aware of my nothingness. The lake behind the garden is a silvery mess, loud crickets and frogs bring the night alive with their lusty cacophony. This solitude I find comforting. The men are gone—the drunkards to the toddy shop, the gamblers to their hangout, the wayward to their women. After twilight's prayers, the zero-watt bulbs come on.

There's a rhythm to every space in this house—the rooms indoors, the outdoors, the spaces in between ... I feel like I am slipping in and out of worlds as I pass through them. This is what the houses in patnam do not have, I remember. In the city, the house is entirely indoors, and once you are out, you are out. There are no spaces that blend the two.

A doctor we visited here told us that we cannot have any children because of my irregular menses. Venkatesan didn't come back home until two that night. When I went looking for him, he was in the temple, saying incomprehensible things in Sanskrit.

When you convinced me to marry him, I told you that we should wait. He gets angry when I read too. He wants me to just exist. Like a sprig of curry leaf, sprinklings of which he can partake of if he needs, never the star of a dish. He has fought with the college and quit his job. Do you know what he does instead? He wears a dhoti, bares his chest and goes to the temple to do the pooja there.

He says he is happiest as a priest. His hair is longer than mine now. How can someone who claims to be so close to god muster so much hate, Subbu?

Sometimes I wake up in the middle of the night with an ache in my being. A pain that does not go away, no matter how much I massage my body with oil, or drink kashayams, dry ginger and palm sugar. It is a pain that has become a part of my soul. Someone said it's a curse upon his family: all of Venkatesan's brothers died before the age of twelve and he should have too, but somehow he survived. And look at us now. On the nights I am whipped, I wonder why the curse didn't work on him. Instead, it feels like, somehow, I am the one who is dead. Are you even alive if you don't see anyone, Subbu? If no one sees you? If you aren't touched or are touching anyone in any sense. If your existence makes no difference to the wheels of the world. When you hide, when you wait, when you lose the will to let the sun catch your eyes, when your hair is a mess, when you do not wash, when you do not speak, when you erase your own self, withdraw from everyone and shrink. Are you alive? I have been hiding. I have called it waiting so far. But waiting is really hiding. Some days I worry that I will die in hiding. That I will go, not even having lived the glorious richness of an ordinary life filled with routines. Like our mother's life. Wake up, make coffee, draw a kolam, water the plants, drink coffee, wash rice, have a bath, pray, cook, feed the birds, rest, have coffee, light the evening lamp, walk to the temple, gossip with friends, come home, eat dinner, go to sleep. The rhythms of her day revolve around the things she thinks are her duty and the things she surrenders to. In between, she makes time for things she likes ... singing every now and then, meeting with her neighbours, going to the astrologer and listening to him say virtuous things about her, or having the woman with the shells predict her future and that of her children's. She likes making matches, taking in relatives who need help getting by, nursing the sick, cursing the noisy. And short cat naps, many of them, knitting in the autumn, fixing the broken, torn and worn. How I long for that life.

I am a woman without a sense of duty. It's because I am without faith. Faith feels like a lost cause when I live like a hostage. If you ask me if there's a god when I am alone, calm, I might say, who knows? Ask me when my hair is in my husband's hands, or when his belt seeks to whip my mind into submission, when his hands grab my head and bounce them off a wall until all of my hair comes undone, when he punches me with both hands, when he uses pain like the farmer uses it on his cattle. Will anyone dare ask me if there's a god in the middle of a beating? Will anyone dare tell me there is one? This is why I have lost my faith. And my sense of duty.

I also feel no need to fix anything. Not even my own self.

If you've ever felt the burning sting of a man's hand across your cheek, as tears of fear and rage fill your eyes and you beg, like a dog, to be allowed to live, it takes a long time to even allow yourself to like who you are. You hate yourself more than you hate him. Why? Why? Why? The question burns away at you. And then why me? And then how? The questions are endless. The answers nowhere in sight. Who will answer? This is not like our Amma's beatings, Subbu. She seemed to hate us girls, but never like this. Not even when she would heat the stalk end of the curd ladle and singe our skin with it. Or when she would pour cold water up our ears and nose to wake us up, or hold us by our hair and dunk us in those cold-water cauldrons. She was angry then, but he seems murderous now. I am surprised by my own resilience, for, many times I close my eyes and think, this is it, now I am going to die. But I seem to keep on living.

Once, in the middle of being hit, I had an out-of-body experience, Subbu. I felt myself leave, and I watched him hit me from the top-right corner of the room. I felt distant. And I wondered why they call a man who is hitting a woman an animal when it looks like the opposite from the outside. The woman is the animal. The one being trained to submit. The man, the one with the whip, is the master. Only when the animal goes mad, wild and, in anger, bites the hand that feeds it will the man run in fear. That day, I found the answer to my escape. I had to bite, bark and run. Like the temple elephant they had to finally set free in the wild when it ran amok, killing men in its wake.

On days when I do nothing, I feel the emptiness of my life. I feel the burden, even when there are no men around to tell me I am one. I am sinking.

I watch others live and I do not burn with jealousy. But a dull throbbing of want rises up from a corner of my heart. I look at them as if they are little girls bonding over candy, carefree. I feel the need to protect them.

Yours,
Lalitha

PS: Hitler, the real one, called Churchill an international incendiary.

It was a while before I realised that the stinging pain I felt on my face was from hot tears. Venkatesan, a man I was very fond of, one who was fond of me and loved me like my own grandfather did, was incapable of any cruelty in *my* world. But this was not my world.

I remembered all the times he offered the sides of his palm to me to bite when I was angry or sad. Some summers, when Amma could not wedge in a week off from work for a holiday, Venkatesan Thaatha came into town. He also loved Amma a lot. She would leave my brother and me in his care. Our father worked away from town for seventeen of the eighteen years I spent in my parents' home. He worked for the state government, and transfer came once every three years.

Amma would pack lunch for us in tiffin boxes, the way she did when we went to school, lay them all out neatly on top of the dining table with a napkin and spoon, just as she did for school, and then go to work. My brother and I would spend most days playing cricket with two brothers, our neighbours. Sunil and Lakshman. One summer, Sunil fractured both his hands while trying to ride the cycle like I did, without holding the handle bar. I spent most of that summer in his house. I read out books to him, because he couldn't even hold *Tinkle*, and we watched *Giant Robo* together. Lakshman was a shy boy who never said much, but could always be counted on to bring fierce competition to the table when we played Business or Snakes and Ladders. One day, Lakshman brought a new Snakes and Ladder game. It was easy to include Sunil in this game because we could roll the dice for him. By some strange stroke of luck, I went from four to hundred on a ladder. I was overjoyed and started to clap and laugh, and Lakshman joined me because he didn't want his brother to win. A livid Sunil exacted revenge by kicking the sheet, coming close to my arm and biting it. Really hard.

I was shocked at first. And then in pain. I ran home weeping. I wanted someone to hurt him as I looked at the deep teeth marks on my hand. Venkatesan Thaatha heard the story, rubbed my face with a towel and wiped all the tears off my face. Then he placed the side of his right palm between my teeth and said, 'Go ahead and bite. Let your anger go, Ammalu.' That's what they called me at home, Ammalu. I kept saying no, but he just kept showing his fleshy palm to me. What I wanted was that he should hurt Sunil. He wouldn't. So I bit him until he bled. He didn't say a thing. Later he asked, 'Okay now? Go and lie down for some time.'

'Die,' I said under my breath, dropping the letter to the floor, fighting back tears. Even though Venkatesan was long dead.

'My friends are coming tomorrow,' Thaatha said. I wiped my face and drank the dry ginger coffee he made for me. 'This will help your cold. Before you go to sleep, rub some dry ginger on your forehead and nose, by morning you will be fine,' he said, stroking my hair.

'Did Lalithamma ever get to sort Venkatesan Thaatha out for what he did to her?'

My grandfather smiled his wry smile, looking just like Amma.

'What use is it discussing the dead? They are gone, erased forever, and I cannot bring myself to feel bad about anybody anymore. I am too old for that, kanna. Anyway, when you were married to someone, there was no time to resolve any problem back then. The way to resolve was to move on, to wake up and treat every day as if the previous did not happen. In those days, in that household, there were many mouths to feed—uncles, aunts, widowed grandmothers, cousins, brothers, their wives and children. So we were busy making food and eating, and I only ever remember the meals anymore, maybe it happens when you grow old, I don't know why … But it was never always horrible or always rosy, you do not just walk around as the sum total of your problems all the time, do you? Time moves you along, and you forget about your problems when you eat a good meal or crack a great joke. With her, we felt as if we were around the most beautiful girl in the planet, her wit made her prettier than she already was. And boy could Lalitha cook. Instead of making her feel confident, her husband, that useless fellow, scoundrel, constantly found ways to make her feel smaller. And he was like that only with her. She married him at an impressionably young age and she saw herself and the world through his eyes. All that was, of course, only until she came to Madras …' he drifted off.

'And?' I asked.

'Not everything was bad always. All would be well for a few months and suddenly something would trigger a fight …'

# 8

# Doors Close. Doors Open.

An old musician friend, Manivannan, a cellist who played for MSV, came to see Thaatha. So I didn't feel guilty leaving him there alone. I had a class to teach at the University. And later my parents were to drop in and stay with him.

'What is this? Saree and all?' Thaatha asked.

'I have a class to teach today. For postgraduate students,' I said, poring over my cyclostyle sheets and making notes between sips of coffee. It was nothing like Saradamma's.

'Gotta get rich. Gotta get a cook,' I said to Thaatha.

'Or wait till you grow old and underpay everyone.' He shrugged.

'I have made dinner, and won't be coming in tonight. There will be enough for lunch. The cornflakes will be on the dining table and milk in the fridge. Please have for breakfast. I'll see you tomorrow evening? Amma, Nana and Arun will be here soon.'

'Okay, madam. Thank you, madam,' he said and pinched my cheeks.

I made Manivannan uncle tea. Just as I was about to leave home, he brought up something I'd forgotten about.

'Some smell is there,' Manivannan said, pointing to a corner of the living room, sheepish and soft, so Thaatha wouldn't hear it.

I was tired of explaining to people that I really didn't smell anything. At first I thought my mother was lying about it to kick me out. And then, when everyone, especially Thaatha, noticed it too, I figured something was wrong with my nose. But I could smell everything. Coffee powder, the kuppa lorry down the road, sambar, Baba's udi in water that Nana gave me when I felt a bit out of sorts, fish on 19B bus, kothamalli, garlic, the stench of railway platforms. So I gave up on trying to figure out what this smell was that others were bothered by. The house loved me, clearly, and never bothered me with it.

I drove down to the University, listening to All India Radio's unintentionally vintage English music programme. At the University, eight students of the thirty-three who had enrolled showed up for class. Of the eight, I knew that only two were interested in sociology. The rest were there for the attendance. After I spoke to a class that looked dead about Indian kinship systems for forty-five minutes, I went on a break. There was always that one student in class who'd Wikipedia-ed her way through the syllabus right at the beginning, and she'd given me hell with her hot takes.

After class, I went to see Saveri aunty, Lalitha's only daughter. I had to see her. Saveri aunty was adopted, it was no secret. Everyone knew about it, it was even in the news when my grandaunt adopted her. She lived in a delightfully quirky house that Lalitha built in Mylapore on a triangular plot. Each floor had only one room but that also meant every room was large and every room had a balcony.

'How long has it been since we met? You are just in time for dinner. I am making vankaya bajji and pachi pulusu.' I watched her burn the brinjal on the flame.

Aunty was what you'd call a handsome woman. There were wrinkles and a few scars, some from chicken pox, one from an accidental brush with a lit incense stick, which caused a Harry Potter-like mark across her left eyebrow, another from a pimple she had picked on. It had the fine stamp of grace, her face. Her hair, a mix of black, brown and grey. She had at last dyed it.

'The last time I went to his college, your cousin's classmate asked him if I was his grandmother. I was furious after that and decided to dye it all black,' she said, and I choked on my coffee.

'I've been telling you to dye it for years now.'

She started greying when she was twenty-five, and my mother claimed it was because, whenever she found a stray grey hair, my aunt would pluck it.

'One turned into five, and by the time she was thirty, she had greyed completely.'

'I know. I know,' Saveri aunty nodded. 'It's a real pain though. I have to wake up early. Put it on. Wait as it drips all over my face, and then wash it all off. And last month, your uncle brought home a dye packet that had expired. After one whole hour spent on this dyeing, waiting and washing, imagine my horror when I looked in the mirror. Every strand still grey.' She showed me a photo from her phone, she looked livid in it.

'You're too much!' My laughter had turned into snorts and coffee was coming out of my nose.

'Stop covering that mouth of yours while laughing. I've been telling you this,' she snapped.

'Ok … Heeee.' I flashed my teeth.

My cousin came home, didn't look around, didn't notice me, went up to his bedroom and locked himself in.

'He will not come out for at least two hours. I know he has a girlfriend. He thinks I don't know. You should see the excuses he makes up. It's as if he thinks we are really stupid.'

'At that age, I remember, even if I was going out with a girlfriend, I wouldn't tell Amma where I was going or to do what,' I said.

'This family is full of pathological liars.'

We sat at the long dining table in the kitchen for dinner. There was a sense of peace in the air. The kind I had felt in Kashi. That didn't last though. In the middle of dinner, Aunty lost her cool, walked over to my cousin's room and banged loudly on the door.

'What?' Varun screamed, flinging the teak door open. He broke into a smile when he saw me.

'Yamuna!' He came and sat next to me.

'So, what were you doing up there?' she asked, winking at me.

'I was in the loo,' he said.

The more we made fun of him, the more lies he made up.

'Did you shave again with your father's razor?' Saveri aunty asked.

'No,' Varun said, more in protest than denial.

'If you shave every day and without proper soap, you will one day shave off all the skin on your face!'

He placed my hand on his left cheek and said, 'I am not hairy like you guys.'

'I remember you were a hairy kid. Wow, Aunty, all your turmeric must have worked on him. Just not on me,' I said, and she broke into giggles.

I settled down for the night on a mattress in Varun's brother's room. He'd moved to America. I could hear Uncle and Aunty talking to each other. Despite the hushed whispers of their conversation, the constant buzzing of Varun's phone and the mosquitoes, I slept well. The next morning, I asked Aunty about her relationship with her parents, trying to sound casual.

'She was more a guru than just an Amma to me, but that wasn't so bad, Yamuna, because she treated her students so well,' Saveri aunty came alive while speaking about her mother. 'Lalithamma took care of us all, her students, just the same. You ask any student of hers and they'll tell you how endless cups of coffee, tea, kashayams and snacks flowed from the kitchen. There was never any dearth for food, you could come anytime and bring anyone along for any meal, no questions asked. It was like a wedding, and she was always the gracious, generous, beautiful hostess. Once, when I was all weepy, a moody teenager, I asked her how she felt when she adopted me, about how she came to love me, to wipe this stranger's child's pee and shit. I'll never forget the way she reacted, I thought she'd rubbish my question or assert that I was her child, and leave it at that. Instead, she caressed my cheeks, and said, "If I can allow a stranger, a grown man into my life, and suddenly call him family, suddenly make serving him my calling, I can allow an outsider, a gorgeous, silken beauty of a babe, to sweep me off my feet, can't I?" She said I taught her true selfless love. When she told me that, I never again felt the need to question anything. How many parents love their own offspring, their own blood, as they say, unconditionally? Selflessly?' She was beaming. 'Since I played the tambura in all her concerts from the age of eight, and sang alongside her in many concerts, I had no doubt that I was indeed her heir.'

I let the beauty of aunt's emotion sink in and drew a sharp breath and asked her about her father.

'Oh? He was a character. I know people like to call him names. I have stopped thinking about him emotionally really, you know? I only remember things that happened from a distance. It's this thing I learnt as a kid. I remember only his jokes. His laugh. The fact that he actually needed me in his last days. Those sort of things. Everything else is a big blur.' And that was all she was going to say. I could tell from the way she had closed up.

'I read a letter,' I said, and she froze.

The silence and the disgust was unbearable. 'I asked him to destroy them years ago. The old man hasn't yet? The nerve …' she trailed off, angry, walking towards the living room.

She called Banaras.

'What? He is in Madras?' she asked the person on the phone, looking at me, her eyebrows raised.

'Thaatha is with me. And he was very careful about what he gave me. Just some light material for my thesis. Research …' I fumbled for words as her face turned pink and her eyes misty.

'Really, Aunty, there was just some stuff about her being unhappy in general. You know? Not having a child … Those kind of things …'

I saw a quick flicker of relief in her eyes as I said that. She softened a bit.

When I reached my parents' home, it was three in the afternoon. I was hungry, but Amma wouldn't let me eat lunch without heating up the rice a little. So I waited around impatiently, plate in hand, in front of the microwave. I'd been spending an extraordinary amount of time with my family the last few weeks, and it seemed like I was always eating. Our meals together simply punctuated an otherwise aimless day.

'If you'd called before coming, I would have kept everything ready,' she said.

'I just decided at the last minute. I slept over at Saveri aunty's house yesterday.'

'I know. She called.' She seemed to want to say something but stopped herself.

'Oh. What did she say?' I asked as I sat on the kitchen counter.

'Nothing, just that you stayed the night. And you said her brinjal was better than mine,' she said.

'I said no such thing. What sambar today?' I jumped off the counter to check, laughing.

'Carrot.'

'Blah.' Instead of the sambar, I had two servings of dosavakkai. 'It's almost over, the avakkai.'

'Yeah, I am wondering if we should even make pickle this year. The monkeys are wreaking havoc on the terrace these days, and in the mango season, they'll go berserk.'

'No! Amma. You have to. I will help. Or come to Chengalpattu and we can do it there.'

Avakkai was among the few things that made the

nothingness of the universe and the meaninglessness of life bearable.

'You could also teach me how to make it then,' I begged.

'Okay, maybe that's a good idea. I'll teach you how to make it the way my grandmother taught me.'

Except for the house, we were pretty much okay with each other. It's funny how much I actually like the woman but hate the things she does.

'Amma, didn't Aunty tell you anything else?' I couldn't handle the tension. I stopped myself from uttering the word 'letter', though.

Amma hadn't expected me to ask her. 'Why are you getting involved in things that have nothing to do with you? My father told me why he's here. Don't act like the upstart that you are with *my* family,' she shot back.

'Is it not mine?' I asked.

'Shut up.' That was that. This was no longer just about the letters.

'This is about the house, is it? Your meltdown? I am not vacating.' I paused before delivering my brahmastra. 'You think you can act like my mother now after abandoning me when I was barely seventeen.'

'Oh come on! You were eighteen. And you'll start about your Barbie doll next,' she muttered, just audible enough so I'd hear it and be reduced to tears.

It worked. Every single time.

'As a matter of fact, I was going to bring it up. What kind of mother gives her child's things away to people who aren't even poor?' I shouted between sobs.

'Don't you feel any embarrassment when crying in front of strangers?' a shrink had asked when I was fourteen.

Until then, it hadn't occurred to me that it was something to be embarrassed about. I wasn't seeing her or anything. She was visiting us, and my mother had asked me to part with a Barbie in a burgundy saree and red bindi as well as a soft beige Teddy bear my father had given me as a sort of joke-gift for my birthday. I'd wanted these all my childhood, but all I got was choppu saaman—tiny kitchen sets and old plywood to play either house-house or teacher-teacher.

Though it was a joke-gift, it meant something to me. I was never close to my dad, but this felt like he was making an effort. It hadn't even been a week since my birthday when my mother's friend, the psychiatrist Comrade Beena showed up, young niece in tow, to consult Amma. That's when Amma forced me to part with my toys. She *had* to conjure up a return gift even when guests arrived unannounced. If she'd been forewarned she would have bought whatever she wanted, but these sudden guests were the bane of my existence. First she forced us, my brother and I, to say 'Namaste' with our hands folded. Then one of us had to sing or play the mridangam. Then she'd serve everyone some sweet and mixture. Just when they were about to leave, she'd press a gift upon the guest. Usually mothers, aunts and grandmothers gave kumkum or betel leaves and blouse bits, but my commie amma wanted to look cool, so she gave cup and saucers or hot packs, or soup bowls, as gifts to women. For men, it was always a shirt bit, and for children some chocolates. For the ones who came suddenly, she'd pluck something that was already a part of our lives to give away. She'd have this weird, creepy grin, shuffling through the shelf, looking for things to give away. My brother started to throw temper tantrums in front of guests, embarrassing Amma, so she stopped taking his and started coming for my things. The Barbie-snatching had reduced me to tears. That's when her shrink-friend asked me that rude question and wrecked any chance that I could discuss this with Amma. They got into a long-winded discussion, right there, in front of me, about the reasons I cried in front of strangers, calling it 'unreasonable'.

'I was only giving away things that you no longer needed, or things that could be of better use to someone else, instead of it just lying around, Ammalu,' she said in a softer tone, and I didn't like it. It's easy to both loathe and love her, but just then, I only wanted to feel the hate in my mouth.

'And making sure I never see you for months? What was that for? You could have sent your precious son to do the house work. Why me?'

'Most young girls that age would thank their mothers for the privacy,' she grunted.

'Privacy in that mofussil town, away from all my friends? What the hell was I gonna do there? Just admit that it runs in your family, this loathing for daughters. Why do you people marry and give birth then if you so hate seeing your own daughters? I read those fucking letters and your family is fucking mental. Primitive and prejudiced shits pretending to be commie egalitarians. That is now my home. I live there. Don't you dare take it from me. I will go to court, I'll sue all of you,' I yelled and stormed out.

'That house is mine. I will do whatever I want with it. And if you think digging up the stench on my aunt is going to help you get that house, you are bloody mistaken.' She slammed the door on me.

'Look, it's history. Let sleeping dogs lie. This is my honest advice.' My father was absolutely useless when I called to ask him for help.

When I reached home, Thaatha was sitting in the living room, watching SVBC channel on mute. Montage shots of the Tirupati temple played back-to-back. He was just staring, not really watching it. To diffuse some of the tension that may have been caused by my letter-stealing, I decided to not speak about it. At all. Instead, once Thaatha was done watching the outside of the temple on loop, I offered him my copy of A.K. Ramanujan's *Relations*. I bookmarked the poem titled 'Prayers to Lord Murugan'. He looked up at me and smiled. He had accepted my offering of peace. I played *Lord Muruga London Muruga*. Seerkali Sivachithambaram's brisk voice brought some cheer into that quiet house.

*In the chambers of my heart, a shrine I have for thee,*
*Come O lord, come O life, come thou dwell in me.*

I wasn't in the mood to cook dinner. So I went down to the bus stop and bought myself a new pack of cigarettes, and parcelled idlis, bajjis and onion chutney. And a few yelakki bananas.

Later, I messaged singer-fanboy Vittal to ask where I could find unverified gossip about the personal lives of Carnatic musicians. He was the one to alert me to a scandal in Lalitha's life after all.

'Rasikas.org.'

Under the Anniversaries and Obituaries section, Smt Lalitha Venkatesan Remembrance Day, a fan had posted the YouTube link to her final concert. She had closed with a Kavadi Chindu in Senchurutti.

Another replied with: 'What great Tamil diction. Nobody to sing like this nowadays.'

'Hello whatabout Sanjay's pronunciation?' someone responded.

'I meant among ladies. Anyway what's with the shonnalum and sheri sheri. Why can't these young singers sing like we speak real Tamil?'

'Does anyone know who started turning all the "sa" sounds into "sha" in Carnatic music?'

'Should not have died the way she did,' SreekarV had posted. He seemed to have killed the thread with his sombre intervention.

What did Sreekar mean by that, though? I Googled every possible thing under the sun, Lalitha Carnatic singer death, Lalitha singer dead, Lalitha Venkatesan Carnatic obituary. Nothing.

That's when I started to suspect that there was something sinister in the way Lalitha died. Was my family covering up something truly ugly?

Later that night, even though I didn't want to look at the letters, I ended up reading a little bit and that's when I noticed what was missing. I'd put it away separately because it was a long letter.

I threw out everything from my closet and searched. There was no sign of the heavy envelope in that debris of kurtas, sarees, old tee-shirts I slept in and Madras-checks shorts.

'I should have read it first!'

Hooks from bras got stuck to my kurta every now and then as I waded through a mountain of cotton and linen. By the end of my search, I was sure that Thaatha had repaid me in kind. I hadn't even left him a note when I took the file from him. Even though I was too ashamed to say anything about it, I was desperate to know.

So I knocked on Thaatha's door and apologised again. 'I really am sorry … I don't know what came over me.'

'You should have asked. I'll be happy to tell you whatever you want to know—'

'As if!'

# 9

# To Patnam

Was it that easy? Would he just tell me if I asked him what I wanted to know. If only I knew what I was after. He seemed to be in the mood to speak, so I let him take me along to his world anyway.

'If you want to know about the past,' he paused for breath, 'You have to also know about the hard times.' Thaatha always sounded like he had a cold, even when he didn't. His voice had changed to a much lower tone as he crossed ninety.

'Hard times like?'

'Our family, it was not easy being a part of such an orthodox family,' he said, biting into a ripe hill banana. 'Their ignorance was harmful to anyone they did not like, anyone who did not follow rules. There was too much pressure on us from old people.' He stressed on the words 'too much' to show just how much pressure he was under as a boy to quit music and take on a more stable career prospect, like teaching or the family business, astrology, which was reading and matching horoscopes. 'That is why I had to run away from the village and join cinema. Cinema for me was a jolly escape, away from those muffs.'

As if to demonstrate just how bad things were back then, Thaatha told me two stories: one about his cousin Balan and another about his niece Malli.

Balan, whom Thaatha had been very fond of, was younger to him by about ten years, and was down with fever that wouldn't go away for weeks. His mother, who didn't believe in English medicine, engaged a traditional doctor to treat the fever.

'That fellow, the rogue doctor, came and set Balan's hands on fire, calling it murattu vaidyam. Some months later, Balan died of the infection on his hand that never healed,' Thaatha said, 'What happened to my niece Malli was worse.'

Malli was born premature and, for the first ten years of her life, Thaatha said, Malli's mother, like a woman possessed, dragged her from masudi to church, temple to ashram, searching for a way to get rid of the evil spirit that had possessed her child.

'Malli could speak very few words clearly but the two words she could say, and she did all the time, was, "Amma, powder". The child, fair and head full of curly hair, never touched a toy, she only played with the tin face-powder dabbas, shaking them and leaving a trail of talcum powder wherever she went. So we called the child "Yardley", and never by her own fragrant name, "Malli". One day, this child simply stopped speaking and no one understood why. We tried our best, bribing her with all manner of cosmetics, but she would not open her mouth. The following week, her mother took her to the lake, tied the child to her saree, and then jumped in,' Thaatha said, and looked at my face, as if to check whether I was horrified enough.

'We did not know for days where the two went, until some men from the neighbouring village fished them out.'

I figured Thaatha intended to disgust me or scare me off with these gory stories, so I would stop digging into the past. But they had the opposite effect on me. I was curiouser than ever.

'This is not what you had in mind when you wanted to revisit the Forties? The past is not the happy place it's touted to be, but the future could be, my dearest,' he tapped on my cheeks gently as if to say 'Enough'.

I wasn't in the mood to let go just yet.

'Won't you tell me about your rebellious youth, Thaatha,' I asked, and his eyes lit up in mischief.

'My life, my youth that's a saga, an epic,' he said in a faux-exaggerated tone, but he seemed to want to talk about something else and not his krantikari days.

'Let me see … What shall I tell you about? Hmmm … Let me see … Ah, shall I tell you about the first movie I saw with Subbu? I think you will like it, it was quite the adventure for your grandma.'

'You first movie date?' I straightened up from my chair.

He grinned and then protested, 'We did not call it date-geet and all back then. It was a simple *outing*, but we took insurance along, a coterie, so we wouldn't be caught in a scandal.'

'Wait, was this outing even before you got married?'

He nodded, 'We went to watch *Kalamegam*, and we had to bribe Lalitha with two cups of ice creams to keep it a secret.'

Google told me the film released in May 1940.

'Correct, correct, that's the year,' he said.

'Where did you watch it, in Chengalpattu?'

He was still smiling. 'No.'

'Here, in Madras? How did you bring her here?'

'All credit to Lalitha only,' he said.

Even as young as three, Lalitha could repeat in pitch perfect tone any tune she heard, Thaatha said. 'Since your grandmother could not trust anyone in that house to actually nurture the girl, she took it upon herself to give Lalitha an education in music. So, Lalitha was sent to the bhagavathar's wife in the next street in Chingleput once every few weeks. Over the next few years, Lalitha's musicianship was so impressive, her grasp of talam so intuitive that the bhagavatar himself, the most popular musician in town, personally taught her music. Then, one day, early in 1940, this bhagavatar in his wisdom recommended Lalitha's name for a concert at the radio station at the big patnam, as Madras was called, and the selection committee approved his recommendation! He went running to their house to tell the girls' father, who thankfully wasn't around. Subbu intercepted him, and told him that her father may not agree to send her sister out alone with him. Now, the bhagavatar, an already nervous chap was worried, he did not want to lose face in front of the committee. He planned to quietly smuggle Lalitha out and steal her back into the house. Nobody would notice her missing in that large house, it was the perfect plan.' He paused. 'Or so they thought.'

'What, they got caught?'

'Worse than that, our singer got cold feet. See, tension before a performance can be too much even for adults, and this was a small girl. The morning of the concert, when

Subbu woke Lalitha up, the first thing she did was cry, and then she said she couldn't breathe or swallow.

'"I won't go alone and sing there. You come, Akka!" she begged your grandmother. Lalitha called Subbu with honorifics like akka and all only when she wanted something done. Subbu was in a fix now. Her father would definitely notice if she went missing, she was his pet after all, so they had to tell him.

'The girls' father, inspite of all the bad-talk from elders, sent them both to the function. Subbu, as always, had managed to convince him. She did so much for that sister of hers, for Lalitha. You know, we all knew that Subbu also longed to study, and to make something of herself, and she could have, if she had been selfish. She always had her father's unconditional approval, but Subbu chose instead to groom Lalitha. Subbu saw the spark in her sister, the makings of a star, long before anyone else could.'

'So when they came to Madras for the concert, you took them all out to the movies?' It was a pretty daring thing to do.

'Yes. After the concert, we ate at the station and went out.'

'To a cinema theatre?'

'No, listen to this.' He wanted to tell this story his way. 'I wanted to take them out to the talkies, but the bhagavatar surprised us all first by saying he had to visit a friend, and requested we accompany him and then he took us to a sprawling bungalow. Subbu, Lalitha and I were stunned by the sheer size of it. I think even the bhagavathar's wife was surprised. We were welcomed into the house by a tall white man and his wife.'

'Who was he, anyone famous?' I asked.

'I don't think so, but he seemed like one of those spiritual types to me. The two of them spoke about this and that, America, war, the Nazis, and all in front of us, but went into another room to discuss something private. You know, for years, Lalitha, Subbu and I made up stories about the two men and what they may have spoken about that day. In one version, they were plotting the downfall of the British, in another, they were exchanging contraband, in yet another, they were Nazis, and in one, they were anti-Nazi agents. This man had a young boy, who came out and greeted us that day. The boy's ayah followed, and kept an eye on us from behind a pillar. All Lalitha said to the boy was "Hallo", but I saw from the corner of my eyes, Subbu couldn't stop smiling. She was bursting with pride, as if Lalitha had recited a sonnet in Queen's English.

'The boy ignored Subbu and me, and took Lalitha's hands into his, and stroked the place her ring finger would have been in. He then looked at her, worried, to check if it hurt. She smiled and then he seemed reassured. Lalitha spoke about this often later. She said everyone, the newspapers, interviewers, the people she ran into every day, her accompanists, husband and child, had a morbid curiosity about her hand. But seldom did they treat it, or her, with the equanimity that boy showed.'

'Was she treated differently because of that hand?' I asked.

'Not in our family, that's all matters, no?' he brushed it off.

'Then you took them to the movie?' I asked, and he nodded.

'I took them out to watch *Kalamegam*, and after the movie we ate peach melba at this place that was your grandmother's favourite after that day, Jaffar's.'

'Did she like the movie?'

'Oh of course, it had Rajarathinam Pillai, her favourite musician, as the hero. And that song that she loved, *Mullai malar naan unakku*. I don't remember much of the movie anymore, but the thing I remember clearly is that this Lalitha kept poking me when a very exciting storm scene was going on. She just did not let me focus. "What did these two men say about Hitler in that house?" she wanted to urgently know. She's obsessed with him, your grandmother whispered to me from the other chair. That man had said, Mahatma wrote a letter to Hitler calling what he was doing to the Jews monstrous. Just a few months earlier, Gandhi had disappointed everyone and said Herr Hitler was not as bad as he was portrayed to be, but he eventually changed his mind. I think, in those years, Lalitha knew more than many a history graduate about that man.'

'Why Hitler?' I was curious.

'I never understood that obsession of hers,' he said.

# 10

# A Blind Date

That storytelling session seemed to have perked up Thaatha's mood. He sang all next morning as I lazed around in the balcony, drinking coffee and reading the paper. It was as pleasant as December was going to get in Chengalpattu. The skies were blue and grey. There was also the rumble of my constant companions, diesel-drunk lorries.

'*Kalyanam, ha ha ha kalyanam* ... It was on the radio today.' Wedding, oh there's a wedding, Thaatha was singing. 'My friend is coming today for lunch,' he said in the middle of the song. 'I forgot to tell you. *Mamiyaar veede sorgathai poley*. A mother-in-law's home is like heaven.' He laughed.

'Which friend?' I asked.

'*Aanukku pennum, pennukku annum, vendum kattayam vazhvile*. A man needs a woman and a woman needs a man in life,' he continued to sing, and then replied, 'One with a writer grandnephew.' An impish smile.

'Offo ... Thaatha, you should have told me earlier, I would have gone to the parlour and got bridal make-up done.'

'Yes, marriage, then kids … How many do you think you will have?' He was laughing again.

'Seven enough, you think? Two sets of twins and one triplet.'

'Tha dhi thang. 2-2-3. Perfectly split.'

I made lunch. This was the first time I was cooking an entire meal for four. Usually it was just me. The scent of coriander, I liked to use a lot of it, and bisi-bele bathed in ghee, reached the postman who came in to deliver a Speed Post.

He asked, 'What special, madam?'

'That boy is finished. He is going to just eat and ask you to marry him right here,' Thaatha joked.

'Pen paarkum padam a?' the postman joined in.

Was this some arranged-marriage trick Thaatha was pulling on me?

'This is not how relationships work now,' I said, and gave Thaatha a crash course on Tinder. He was more excited than I expected him to be. And wanted me to show him how the app worked. And nearly recognised some boy in there as a relative. Thaatha tried to get me to do a left, right, left pattern, and then made me show what the men see.

'How different is it from looking at a girl once before marrying?' he asked.

'They don't marry. They meet for fun.'

'Fun? Games and stuff?'

'Well …'

Saved by the bell! I let Thaatha answer the door. His friend looked younger than him, and the writer looked like he hadn't shaved in months. I could tell he was embarrassed by it because (a) Thaatha was clean-shaven, as was his grandfather, and (b) he kept touching his beard every now and then as if mentally willing it to disappear.

'I am a very good friend of your grandfather's. Govindan,' he said, emphasising the 'good' the way only older men did.

'Of course … I have heard you perform so many times,' I said. Govindan, nadaswaram vidwan, was so legendary that there was a hall named after him in the heart of the city while he still lived. Usually, these honours were reserved for the dead in musical circles.

'He was the foremost player of his time. Sheer genius,' Thaatha said. He held Govindan's hands in his own. It was sweet.

'His son is the reigning king now,' Thaatha said.

Govindan waved his hands as if he didn't approve of all this praise. 'Your grandfather has done a lot for musicians, ma. Before he founded the union, we were being ripped off by those rich movie producers who stole our tunes,' he said. 'You know who introduced us? Your chithi paati. Lalitha.'

They both made that wistful face. One that I'd seen everyone make when talking about Lalitha. Dead and gone, their lips seemed to say.

'What naadam she had no, pah?' he asked Thaatha, who nodded and sighed. 'What music hers was. Intuitive. Uninhibited.'

That was the word everyone used while talking about her: uninhibited. Did Thaatha invite this friend so we could talk about Lalitha? Was this a peace offering for taking the letters back?

Govindan then pointed to his companion, 'This is my sister's grandson, Karthik.'

'Hi.' That was the shortest hello possible.

'Hey,' I said and went in to get them some water.

He was awkward and wanted to leave before lunch, but the two old men asked him to stay. I was angry when Thaatha made up ludicrously old-fashioned lies, grinning foolishly: 'She has been cooking for hours. Just because you, you both I mean, would be coming. She is a great cook. You shouldn't miss it. It's so difficult to make elaneer payasam.'

I said, 'There's no compulsion. You can leave. I will drop your grandfather back wherever.'

That seemed to ruffle him a bit. 'No. No. No. No …' Karthik protested. His ears had turned scarlet. 'I'll stay for lunch.'

'Back in the day, for your information, this Kannaiya and I ate anything that walked, crawled and flew,' Govindan said.

Thaatha was laughing his hearty laugh, one that made his eyes small and sparkle. 'Of course, he does not eat now, having moved to Banaras. It was hard for me, watching him go through everything alone. Subbu was such a wonderful woman. A great cook … I am glad I saw you before you left town,' he said.

Karthik, who was quiet until then, asked, 'So what do you do?'

'Doing a PhD. I think.'

'Oh?'

I told him what I'd been doing.

'You should tell me more some time.'

'Sure. What do you want to know?'

'He said "some time". Which means you should meet him outside and tell him about it,' Thaatha said, and his friend patted Karthik and winked at him.

'No, no. I mean. I was just saying …' He blushed again.

'It was small talk,' I helped him out, gritting my teeth, glaring at Thaatha.

'Why did you choose this area though?' he asked.

'I am not sure. Maybe it chose me,' I said and then realised how stupid I sounded. 'That sounded stupid and cheesy. It's just that, with Thaatha and a Carnatic singer grandaunt, there was no way I could have not done this.'

'Not stupid. Not cheesy,' he smiled.

Our grandfathers finished their meal, got up and went into the living room.

'Can I read it, whenever it's ready?'

'Hah, I have no idea which way my research is headed. It's been driving me crazy. I will tell you more another day.' I smiled and he smiled back. He was handsome. A thick mop of straight hair fell on his face, covering his forehead. And then there was the beard. I wondered what it would be like to kiss him. I had never kissed anyone with a full beard.

'You are a writer?'

'I am,' he said confidently, the way only someone who had published a book already could.

'What do you write?'

'My second novel will be out soon. I write crime fiction. Historical,' he said.

'Oh. What's the first one called?'

'*Treasures of Trivandrum*.'

'Oh.' I suppressed my sarcasm, and decided to not judge him until I had read the book. 'I would really like to read yours.' He said he'd give me a signed copy later and had two servings of the payasam. 'Thanks. I haven't had this great a meal in a while. I live alone here and my cooking isn't the best.'

'You can come here anytime for a meal if you want to,' I said, and then realised that was a bit much.

'I'll possibly take you up on that,' he said, looking away, awkward.

The two friends were deep in conversation in the living room.

'Would you like some tea?'

'Yes. Shall I help?'

'You just said your cooking sucks, let me make it,' I said.

'Hey, it doesn't suck ... But yeah, well.'

I made my famous ginger tea, and we sat in the balcony watching the traffic go by in the distance on Bypass road.

'This place used to be so quiet,' I said.

'I can imagine,' he said. 'Have you lived in Madras all your life?'

Usually, when someone asked me this, I wanted to do two things: scream or disappear. It sounded simple enough, but when they asked, I felt their probing eyes on me. As if they were sizing my worth up. My life's experiences were all trapped in one city—and not even the biggest city in the country. It left an ugly aftertaste in my mouth, this question. As if the other person thought poorly of my life and my views on lofty things. As if it were all to be discounted, because just what do you know of life if all you know is your home? I was a kenathu thavalai. At first I pitied myself for my stupid frog-in-a-well life. Then I felt the resentment and rage build up. First against my parents, of course, poor things. And then at the world for being so inaccessible to me. And then the person who posed this question. For that hint of arrogance. I have lived only here because I cannot afford anything else. I cannot afford to live and study in a different city or country. Okay?

Weirdly enough, the way he said it didn't offend me. Also, he immediately followed it up with, 'You have to show me around. I haven't made many new friends here.'

'Will do,' I smiled my polite-stranger smile.

We drank our tea quietly after that.

After tea, I tried to break the silence. 'I have heard your grandfather so many times.'

'Oh nice. I am not so big on Carnatic music,' he said.

'Oh? Have you heard Lalitha?' There's got to be a reason Thaatha introduced me to him. I wondered if he too was like Vittal.

'Ummm ... never, actually. I'll be honest with you. I don't get it. I don't know how to put this to someone who's an insider-outsider like you. But I think of Carnatic music as a square, you know ... Like a box. It's just ... too inaccessible to me. Even to enjoy it, you need to know so much. And it's a very closed space, even for someone who just wants to listen.'

'You speak to our grandfathers, and they'll tell you this music was everywhere, sung by everyone. I was reading an interview of Rajarathinam Pillai, and he talks about how therukoothu, harikatha, nadodighoshti, all of these made Carnatic music the default songs of the masses. All of that is marginalised now, which is possibly why it's so alienating. It's become a polarised, elitist space now.'

'You really have thought about this, huh?'

'I haven't. Rajarathinam Pillai has though. So, what do you like?'

'I like random music. Movies. Some old bands. Things like that. Nothing fancy. I love Mali's flute though. Now, that feels accessible.'

'When he plays Magudi—' I began, and he burst into life instantly.

'Oh my god, yes. My grandmother wouldn't let us play that song of his at night. She'd say a snake was sure to come home listening to Mali play it on his bamboo flute. It was a folk snake-charmer's tune, after all!'

When his grandfather called out to him, Karthik got up and then asked for my number. 'I'll give you a missed call,' he said and went out.

I saved his number and closed the door. Thaatha, as always, didn't ask me anything. Instead, he went to the bedroom and started packing for his return the day after.

I sat on his bed, and asked, 'Why can't you just stay here?'

'You know why.'

I left the room when I noticed there was a WhatsApp message.

'It was great meeting you. How does a coffee sound? The day after. Tomorrow I have a meeting with my local editor and it may take long.'

'Coffee sounds good.' Thaatha who was standing behind me, broke into that song.

*Kalyanam, ha ha ha kalyanam …*

And then I knew why he had been singing about marriages all day long. I was a bit confused even then though. Karthik for sure was not from 'our community'. Had Thaatha come all the way here to arrange this encounter? Why was he crossing the Lakshman Rekha of caste now, for this match?

I turned around, 'One date, and you are already planning my wedding?'

'Sometimes all it takes is one look.'

'Was it? Was it love at first sight for you? You have got to me tell me before you go, Thaatha.'

# 11
# Thaatha's Tale of Subbu

*She was a distant cousin, so no, it was not love at first sight. Her great-uncle introduced me to the audience when I went to Chingleput to give a concert. I saw her in the crowd. Her smile, it started from her curving lips and spread until her eyes lit up. Her cheeks—they looked as if she had stuffed two big laddoos in them when she smiled. I knew her, of her, for long, from the time she was born, actually, and I met her in Madras, and we'd even watched a movie together already, remember? This was a month or so before that.*

*Subbu had rebelliously curly hair that she tried to rein in with oil. She was broad-shouldered, big-made, beautiful and had presence. It was hard to ignore her. When we spoke about that day later, yes, we did speak about it, she remembered what I wore and what she thought of me. She said, I was handsome, but not handsome like the boys of her village. The ones who had toned upper bodies and played badminton. She too played badminton, you know, until our wedding, wearing long pavadais. I was shocked by how bold she was. This was before we even got married, she told me I was handsome in a way that made me 'seem' rich; I wasn't. Discontinuing school at fourteen, I'd run away from home and joined a cinema company.*

*I watched her from the stage as I sang, and she fidgeted because she knew I was looking.*

*She was no delicate damsel, your grandmother. It sounds silly saying this now, but at that time, Subbu was the only unmarried fourteen-year-old in the entire family, some girls her age were even pregnant.*

*Subbu was the one who convinced her father to send Lalitha to school even after she came of age. Potta kozhi koovi pozhudu vidiyadhu. That's what her father said, it doesn't dawn when a hen crows, no, it only dawns when the rooster crows, so why should these hens want to strut around in schools? But all the men in that house did was fatten up like goats ahead of Eid, while the women cooked and cleaned and sewed and birthed. So, all the men went to school, but the women of the house, none of them did. Despite feeling that way, her father sent Lalitha to school because Subbu had asked it of him.*

*That day, the concert went on until seven in the evening, but she had to be home before sunset. When I went back to her house, she came running to the courtyard and offered me water to wash my feet. When her father turned around to go into the other room, and there was no one but us, I took the rose garland that was given to me at the concert and handed it to her. She ran into the kitchen, not before snatching the garland from my hand.*

*Subbu is why I found success, and she's certainly why Lalitha found success, she was our coach. She was a happy, selfless, joyous woman, devout, sharp, dutybound. She ruled our lives like an empress. You know how some people arrive fully made, as if they are grand, old souls? She was like that. Your mother used to joke that Subbu sat in her chair the way Queen Victoria does on her throne. While on her deathbed at the hospital, a new nurse tried to chat Subbu up and asked her, 'Paati what's your name?' And Subbu smiled, 'Victoria.'*

# 12

# Good Men and Bad

When I finished reading Karthik's book that night on Kindle, I didn't want to seem too desperate. So, I didn't message him about it. Instead, I logged on to Facebook to look for him. We had seventeen common friends. Surprisingly, he hadn't added me after going home. I would wait for him to send a request, I told myself. That resolve lasted two minutes.

Then I Googled him and read all the ecstatic and less-than-enthusiastic reviews that his book had received. Despite the title and the terrible Nineties-type windows clip-art cover, the book had been very, very entertaining and well written. I was already impressed.

The next day, as I was getting into the car, my phone dinged with a WhatsApp message.

'Horrible meeting with editor. The only thing left to look forward to now is our coffee tomorrow. How does 7 p.m. sound?'

'Sounds good. And hope the day gets better.'

'It just did!'

He was better at flirting over text. We decided on a place that served good filter coffee and would allow us to sit for a little extra while. I did not tell anyone about the place because I didn't want it to become crowded. I went home from University and helped Thaatha pack up the rest of his things. He combed his hair, said some prayers and napped on the easy chair for a while.

'You didn't leave the house at all,' I said to him.

'So what? That's the best thing about old age. Everyone comes to see you,' he said. 'I am exhausted just at the thought of going out and talking to people here.'

At the airport, he held my hand. 'Remember what Chandrababu sings in *Kalyanam*, man needs a woman but also vice versa.'

I groaned. We shared a plate of sambar vadai at Sangeetha and drank coffee. It was a particularly windy day. No crowd near any of the gates, just the guard whistling every few minutes at speeding taxis.

'Thank you, Thaatha.' I didn't want to say sorry again. So, I thanked him, he heard the sorry in it anyway.

'With age, you learn to act patient.' He patted my cheeks and sat in the wheelchair, and the airport staff whisked him off to check-in.

'One minute, I almost forgot!' I ran behind the wheelchair. I fished out from my bag the camera phone I'd bought online for Gopal.

That smile. 'You remembered. Good girl,' he said, his eyes sparkling, shaking my hand. I felt like a little girl who'd earned a star for her homework. When he left, I wanted to go with him to Banaras. I would soon enough, I told myself.

There was some more time before my rendezvous with the writer. So I went to meet a friend. Kavita lived a few minutes away from the restaurant Karthik and I were meeting at. I told her about Thaatha's visit, and she asked if I could help her mother plan a trip to Kashi. When I told her mother that she could stay with my grandfather, and that he would handle all the arrangements, she took my hand in hers. 'This sort of thing doesn't happen to everyone, you know? We are lucky,' she said.

Just the idea of going to Banaras brought out in the devout this sense of sobering gratitude. Like someone one knew had just died and woken everyone around to their own mortality.

I told Kavita, whom I'd known since school, about ending things with Sundar.

'Five years must be some sort of record for him. And it's because you should have left him long, long ago. You're a masochist.'

'I know. But it's all good now,' I assured her.

It was all good because we had blocked each other out completely. From Facebook, Twitter, on the phone. He was gone from my life, in reality and on the internet.

Ten minutes after pretending to be totally fine, Kavita broke down.

She'd gone out drinking to a bar with a long-time mutual friend, Kiran. They'd then bounced from one bar to another through the night, and had ended up at a nice hotel around two in the morning. It was the last stop, and it's where she was friends with the bartender. Everywhere else, she was friends with the wait staff. Not anyone from the kitchen or behind the bar. The staff loved her. She tipped well, and she knew that it was a sure-shot way of keeping her seats safe at bars. Kavita would only have to sit for the mojitos to magically appear at her table. And then, when these men quit one bar, and went to manage another, she'd go there too, and corner their best tables and complementary starters.

Kavita drank one too many mangoritas, 'which is really like a naughty liquid Mango Bite', she explained. The handsome barman always spotted her around the bar table, and handed her the drink, no matter how sweatily crowded with rich people the counter was. Even if VIP clients were waiting for their drinks, Kavita wouldn't have to. It was the bartender's invention, the mangorita, and she loved it. And he loved that she loved it so religiously. So, he poured her at least five generous, boozy Maazas.

Kavita ended up spending the night with him. Him, not the barman, that would have been epic. And worth it, instead she ended up with criminal Kiran.

'The fucker stealthed me. He literally shushed me in the middle of sex, when I realised he wasn't wearing a condom.'

She was not crying. I watched her. Her voice wasn't shaking. Just angry.

'Why the fuck would they fucking ban the morning-after pill in this state, di? Ah, I fucking hate this village.'

Should we report him to the police for rape, I wanted to ask her. But I knew what she'd say, and the thought of my friend being humiliated in court by a creepy judge maama was less than inviting. We made discreet enquiries on WhatsApp but couldn't just wait around for people to reply. So the two of us hopped on to her scooter and scouted around hospitals and medical shops in RA Puram, feeling sweaty and embarrassed under the smirks of young boys and disapproving glares of older women at the shops. Finally, after a lot of furious WhatsApping, we found a shop that sold it to us on the black. We didn't care what the mark-up was, but we asked the shopkeeper a hundred times if it was safe. We Googled a lot, read up on its ingredients and then she finally popped the pill right there in the middle of the road.

She popped the pill and laughed in a slightly scary, deranged, Balachander-movie-heroine way. 'Idula, my mother wants me to get married this year. She's found me some boy.'

I suspected then that we were both a bit unhinged in our own way. It's all that pressure to get married.

I drove from Kavita's home to my date, exhausted and numb. At a signal, I checked Kavita's Facebook and Instagram. She hadn't blocked Kiran. So I also didn't.

He hadn't gone in to the restaurant. And when Karthik saw me reversing, he made a thumbs-up sign. It was a nice day to sit al fresco, and that's saying something in Madras. The sun seemed a bit preoccupied, thankfully, and the wind was a steady presence.

This was my spot—a junction where the traffic was sparse, but steady enough that I could catch an auto should something go wrong with my car. Some women selling flowers and vegetables always sat outside, so I didn't feel weird sitting alone by the road, drinking coffee.

Mary, the vegetable lady, waved some fresh-looking pudina at me. I made a dosa-flipping hand gesture, to mean I'll come later. She shrugged and went back to sprinkling water on her greens.

'Hey.'

'Hi. Before we go in, can I ask you something?'

'Um, yeah.' What was this now?

'Can this be our first date? So we can forget about what our grandfathers have done?'

I laughed. 'No … I think it's sweet what they did, come on!'

The waiter asked, 'Horlicks. Sambar vadai-ya?'

Karthik's eyes widened in horror. 'Mini coffee.'

'Horlicks?'

'The bhavans make really good Horlicks,' I tried to explain.

The horror lingered for a few more seconds. 'Anyhoo … I went home and stalked you on Facebook and realised we have some crazy number of common friends. How do you know Daniel?' he asked.

'Danny was my school-dash-auto friend between classes three and five. How do you know Vinod?'

'We went to the same IIT preparatory class … Both Danny and Vinod are in the US now,' he said.

'Who isn't? Either working in America, or married to someone there. I have like one friend left in town now.'

'I don't mean to be frivolous, but is that how you know I am friends with Vinod, because you also stalked me?'

'I sent you a friend request after I finished reading your book,' I said.

'What?' He took his phone out. 'Sorry.'

He didn't want to talk about the book, it looked like. I persisted anyway. 'You write really well. I was so impressed with that twist in the temple priestess's past.'

He looked away and tried to smile. Do writers not know what expression to wear when you compliment them, or was it just our man that didn't?

Karthik and I had more in common than I thought

we did. We spoke about this and that, music and films, and he gave me a laundry list of movies to watch. And as most film conversations tended to in my world, ours too found its way to Ilaiyaraja and Rahman. All this as the waiter hovered around our table. He finally lost patience when I began to hum a song rather terribly, and asked, 'Can I bring the bill?'

Karthik walked with me to the car. We were the exact same height. Even our hands were the same size. He was as old as I was, and I couldn't believe that, where all my friends had failed, and all the apps had failed, our thaathas had shone.

I opened the car door, expecting him to say something or that we'd at least peck. That didn't happen. I got in, waved him goodbye and stepped on the clutch when he knocked on the window.

I lowered the glass.

'Now that you know I am sane sober, can we go get a drink the next time?'

'I was beginning to wonder if you were a teetotaller,' I said.

Saveri aunty sent me an audio file with a laughing-crying smiley that morning on WhatsApp. Baby maama, who'd retired as a high court judge a few years ago (and whose real name was Ramanathan but none of us called him that), had taken on the role of the family genealogist. He was reading from his mother, acid-tongue Alamelu's autobiography every day, and sending recordings to his cousins. Alamelu-the-legend, that's what Amma called her aunt, was a freedom fighter who ran away to Gandhi's ashram and only returned on the promise that she could study further. One her mother-in-law had to make in the presence of Madeleine Slade.

# 13

# Mrs Alamelu's Story

*Dear family, hello, this is Baby. It is my late mother Mrs Alamelu's birth anniversary this month. In honour of the lady who fought for a free India and for women's rights all her life, I have decided to read her autobiography to all of you. I have been sending one chapter a day for the last week, and I have heard and enjoyed all your comments.*

*This is a chapter that I hesitated to send, but after discussing with my daughter Rama and my wife Mrs Rajarajeshwari, I have decided to send it to you. Now, I understand it may cause some consternation among certain sections of the family to hear this, especially the language. I request you to take it as a historical record and nothing more, and not as a commentary from me on anyone's parents or grandmothers. I feel compelled to give this chapter a U/A rating as they do in cinemas for strong language.*

*I begin from page number fifty-four, chapter nine of I Dream for My Sisters, the Autobiography of Alamelu:*

*When I turned twelve, I knew the time for my marriage was not far away. But luckily for me, my parents took their time—two years to be precise—in finding me a match. I was broader than other girls my age, even my cousin Subbu, who was quite broad. I thought that's why my well-to-do in-laws picked me from all the matches that had been lined up for my husband.*

*The first wedding I remember vividly is my cousin Subbu's. For forty-five days after she heard Kannaiya play at a concert in Chingleput, every morning, Subbu went to the small Pillayar temple under the banyan tree by the canal with a hand-woven garland. Her sister Lalitha and I accompanied her. She prayed to God that harmonium genius, Comrade Kannaiya, and she be brought together in marriage. Her father knew how she felt, and I had a feeling he approved too. Which is why it didn't surprise me when, suddenly, he decided to arrange her marriage.*

*My mother didn't allow me to touch her much, and this only seemed to get worse when I got my menses. Meenakshiamma, who was in charge of bringing up all the girls of my age, was our big heartbreak. She did not allow us to talk back to the men of the house. Certainly not to the boys we went to school with. She did not allow us to go out the door on most days. And when the girls in the house had their menses, she scolded them so badly that they spent those three days cursing and crying in the backyard. There were no exceptions, her own daughters, Lalitha and Subbu, were subject to the same caustic rage.*

*Meenakshiamma (who was not widowed then) ganged up with the old widows, who had all shaved their heads, wore kavi sarees, and used bad words to mindlessly hurt the virgin girls in the house who were menstruating every month.*

*'How conveniently you have got your period right in the morning so you can do no work all day. Whore. I curse that you get married on a Friday and return the following Saturday widowed. Bald and sandal smeared over your head.'*

*'Die in that corner. The year you were born, we lost so many people like flies. We should have known just then how inauspicious you were.'*

*Or 'You swallowed your mother just as soon as you were born'.*

*Or 'You came wiping all our wealth clean from your mother's womb'.*

*Or 'You came out tearing your mother down there, right then we knew you'd turn out like this'.*

*Or 'You're destined to die a virginal widow'. Sometimes they called the girls 'whoring widows'.*

*How and why the women of my family cursed so much, I never figured out. Most of it involved becoming a widow. They had a song-like tune for each of the curses. Parvatamma told me that the women who cursed were raised by a particularly foul-mouthed ancestor. 'That woman spoke only bad words. Ammama,' Parvatamma said, tapping her mouth with her fingers, making an 'O' with her lips.*

*I did not understand how Parvatamma tolerated our home and its always-angry women. She was employed to wash the brass vessels and clothes. The sound of clothes being thrashed against the stone informed us all that it was time for noon coffee. She came twice a day. Parvatamma also helped my grandmother with her business, selling curd, butter and vegetables. And she washed the old, bald bodies of men and women in the house. She got a round of leftovers along with us children. She told me her arms ached in the night and that she could not sleep until she had massaged her body with hot oil. It was all the washing ... the brass vessels, the fat or bony ancestors of mine.*

*You must always find ways to tell your family that they are wrong. I did get my revenge on all these women and men. When I started getting my menses, for three months I hid it from everyone. Coming and going everywhere as I pleased, defying them, taking part even in homams and festivities, delirious in my secret. Until, one day, my father saw me washing my stained clothes by the well, and told everyone, howling in the courtyard. How he and my amma had beaten me then.*

*That's when my wedding was fixed. I was fourteen then. My mother was eight when she was married. She came with seven trunks of gold they said. And was so special to her mother that she was fed the pearls of ladies fingers fried in ghee every day for her afternoon snack. In this house, she rarely left the kitchen. She was cooking from dawn till noon. So when they arranged my marriage, I had little hopes of ever being able to leave the kitchen.*

*By today's wedding standards, mine was a simple affair, not as crowded, but it was still seven days long. At the welcoming ceremony for the groom's family, Chingleput's most popular nadaswaram party arrived in style. Guests came from all the villages nearby, from our side and the groom's side. The entire house was decorated with mango leaves tied up together as a thoranam. My aunts spent an entire week ahead of the wedding in the backyard, husking rice, singing and working hard.*

*We hated weddings because one of us unlucky girls was always made to grind chutneys or the batter for vadai or adai. We'd have to grind them on the stone mill for hours, and our hands would burn from touching those red and green chillies all day long. After we made the chutney, we had to soak our hands in warm water for hours while everyone else took part in the festivities. We couldn't have a bath or even go to the bathroom without Parvatamma's help then. I remember trying to have a bath once by myself and my body burnt, it was like I had bathed in chutney. I was on fire and no amount of coconut oil or buttermilk on my skin would help. I had to jump into the kolam in the temple to help the burning sensation, and stayed there for an hour.*

*Since it was my own wedding, I was spared the chilli treatment. I saw poor Lalitha with her hands in a bowl of warm water the entire day of my wedding. After the tying of the thaali, I could not stop my tears as my new family took me away. I was being carried by my nana to the horse-drawn jhatka waiting outside. My twenty-nine-year-old husband, whose first wife had passed away giving birth to their third son some months ago, took me in his arms at the entrance and bundled me into the vehicle.*

*As the horse carriage started to move, my father said to my mother-in-law, 'How quickly girls turn into women.'*

There wasn't much about Lalitha in this audiobook, but I figured it was Saveri aunty's way of asking me to not give up. She never said it, of course. Over the course of the next weeks, she sent recipe books handwritten by my grandmother and an old audio recording of my grandfather singing Tony Brent's *Game of Love*.

It seemed to me like she, too, was looking for something. What did this family do to Lalitha?

# 14
# Iqbal Bano and Faiz

My next date with Karthik was at his friend's place. We had planned to get a drink at the Ranjith rooftop, but he had a party to go to.

'I would love it if you came along,' he said.

I agreed, even though conversations with strangers in intimate settings gave me stomach ache. I always end up having a good time, but just the thought of getting dressed and going out made me want to not do it.

'So, how do you guys know each other?' Asha, the birthday girl, asked me at the party.

'Our grandfathers are friends.' I smiled.

'How romantic.' She offered me banana chips, the attentive hostess. The taste of the coconut oil it had been bathed in lingered long after I was done with the chips. As did some of the chips that were stuck to my upper teeth. There really was no elegant way to get rid of it. I tried to wash it down with a drink. That didn't work either. And yet I couldn't stop eating the chips.

'So, what do you do?' I asked her, resisting the urge to pluck the bits wedged between my teeth with my bare fingers.

'She is in the country on vacation,' Karthik said to me, and turned to his friend and said, 'She is a researcher,' introducing me to her.

'Oh, you are?' she said. 'I am on a break from work. So …'

We clinked glasses. She did not ask me about work. I was okay with that. I didn't ask her about hers, she didn't seem to want to talk about it anyway.

Asha's apartment had a laidback vibe. A warm yellow glow washed over everything. The room was lit thoughtfully. Lamps at an angle from the ceiling. Floor lamps with LED bulbs inside, strings of fairy lights hung on the balcony just around the corner. It was something someone young, with their own space and extra cash in hand could do. Spend time on the lighting in their home. Even the bathroom had a warm glowy yellow tubelight. In my homes, both in Chengalpattu and Madras, every room had one kind of tubelight. White and bright. If the fuse blew, we bought another one. Just the same. White and bright. No other light would do. The older people in my house had lived through zero-watt bulbs and bad yellow lights for long and treated them with a sort of contempt. Like we had brought the streetlights in. My mother didn't let me change the lights in Chengalpattu even. Anyway, I didn't have much money to spare on décor on my measly government research grant.

There were plants inside this house. Nice, long, healthy leaves. No dust on them. None dead or in various stages of samaadhi, like in my house. No doubt there were people employed to dust. Dust between the books in the huge library that wasn't covered with a bedsheet or a glass door like we did to shut the door in the face of dust mite. Just clean surfaces. Under the sofa, behind the rosewood and wicker chairs, in the crevices of the dining table.

Everyone looked polished. I did too, to be fair. I had blow-dried my hair and got a mani-pedi. I didn't look out of place. But everyone's clothes had this sheen. They looked regular, yet something about them said not-regular. Like the mild shimmering silver saree with a bold red sleeveless blouse that the host was wearing. Something I'd ogle at on the Raw Mango Instagram page, hoping that, if I stared at it long enough, the universe would conspire in bringing me together with it. Well, this party looked like a Raw Mango ad on steroids. Everyone looked not just rich, desi rich. The cutlery and the plates were all desi rich too. You know, paisley prints with golden rim, elephants and Mughal-inspired designs right in the centre. The spoons were silver. Actual silver. Not ever-silver. And even the glasses out of which we drank water and wine were ornamental. The only kind of glass I had? Tumblers. Steel tumblers. If some very rare guests came, my mother would with much showmanship whip out the peengan cups or glasses for tea or kheer.

I didn't know if I loved or judged this party. Maybe I was just a little jealous. I made a mental note of every aesthetic the room presented me with. As if I wanted to rip it all off and make my own cheap version at home. Maybe I can stitch this blouse with my Mani Tailors if I buy the material from Sowcarpet. Maybe I can buy plastic wine glasses like this online for cheaper. Maybe I can just pick up fairy lights by the metre from Richie Street for a fraction of what they possibly spent. The food at the party was elegant desi too. Flaky parottas that fell apart as soon as they hit the tongue. Kababs. Biriyani. Mirchi ka saalan. Whole steamed fish in banana leaves. A fruit custard. And carrot halwa. And the music was lovely. Just mellow and innocent. Like the beginning of an easy romance.

'How is it? Living away from home?' I asked Asha.

First she sighed. Then she thought about it for a few seconds. 'It's like, you try so hard and then you get into one of these foreign universities and you think that's it. You're set. You are not,' she said. She was petite, with a crew-cut, and her big nose ring caught the fairy lights every once in a while.

'But it really gives you a chance to meet a terrific number of people who share your own sort of stories.' She paused for a sip. 'And even a person with the slightest curiosity, the sort of curiosity we are all brought up with about other places, in a local there, about you, makes them a non-racist Indophile in your eyes. It's weird. It's nice sometimes. But mostly you're just in limbo and are always a bit on the edge. Like you have to be on your best behaviour, or the hostess will think you are a bad guest. Never know what will be used against you to deny you a visa.'

'So, I was once in Barcelona,' her boyfriend Ameer, who was drinking a mojito, said, 'which by the way is teeming with Indians and Pakistanis selling souvenirs and running supermarkets all over, especially Las Ramblas, when I met this desi man. He asked us how we got a Spanish visa. When we told him we applied for a Schengen from a different country, he said, "I want someone from my family to visit me and I have not been able to bring them in for twelve years now because they think he may not leave." Imagine not being able to meet your brother for over a decade because you're second-class.'

'Fuck immigration,' Asha said.

Karthik pitched in: 'I'm a Schengen reject. I didn't have enough money apparently. They need a lot more proof that brown people will not permanently squat.'

'The good news is, I hear, it's not that easy for anyone to come to India either. They're strict about who can come and live,' someone said, and while that would have made us laugh earlier, because you'd think 'serves white people right', everyone in the room had something else on their minds then. Something we hadn't spoken about.

Asha decided to change the music. She opened YouTube and just as the song began, the air in the room seemed to shift. Slowly. The violin, tabla, 50,000 people from Lahore, and a defiant Iqbal Bano reached out to us from 1986. By the time she reached '*sab taj uchhale jayenge*' the entire party had gathered around the speaker, as calls of 'Inquilab Zindabad' pierced the night.

Songs of revolution replaced even happy birthdays in the December of 2019 in many a street, home and bagh. One had to be in that crowd to finally feel what one had only read about. To hold the tricolour under the eyes of a state that viewed every fist held out high as seditious.

When the song ended, I walked out to the balcony where it was quiet. I lit a cigarette and looked up. The crescent of the moon looked upon the balcony benevolently, and the occasional breeze played hide-and-seek with wisps of hair that had begun to rebel from my ponytail. Down the road, a few cars sped into the horizon.

Everything was a wine-soaked blur. Madras was beautiful in that moment. Karthik joined me just then. We smoked in silence.

When we went back in, the visa conversation was still on. On the speaker, Shubha Mudgal was melting into *Bagiya lahoo luhan, Hariyali ko ankhen tarse.*

Out of what I thought to be politeness, Ameer asked me if I'd ever considered leaving India for good. Asha made a sound that was a vocal approximation of her irritation with the question.

'I am going back to Muscat, I've found me a job,' he explained. He grew up there and his civil engineer father had just retired and moved back home to Thalassery.

'I mean, I can't leave, I think. I have nowhere to go really,' I started and then the old word vomit started to come out of my mouth. 'Passport-changing is like the creation of a new order, don't you think? Devised to make some people with their dark skin and different-coloured passports somehow inferior.'

'So you think I should just be here, read the news, follow court proceedings and wring my hands in horror over pogroms as the threat of my citizenship being stripped away becomes more and more real? And if a mob lands up at my door, calling my marriage to my girlfriend an act of jihad, what then? The nerve you have to judge us?' he asked, his voice calm, pointed. The room turned quiet as a ghost town. Slowly, everyone slinked away from me. I understood what that conversation was really about.

I apologised or tried to, and fumbled. 'Sorry, I didn't realise we were still talking about NRC. I'd love to go off and live in some Sweden-type place. I can't see how though.'

Ameer then proceeded to shock me by putting his arm around my shoulder, and he joked, 'It's okay, machan. I get it. You are a mofussil chick.' That had both of us in splits, and he went on, 'Don't have any foreign connections? You're not posh like me, no? Go ahead and resent me.'

'Sorry,' I mouthed to Karthik. He shrugged, I think he was embarrassed of me for a bit there.

After this, both of us drank more. Anita tried to change the air in the room with a Telugu item song. Ameer and I danced with a bottle of vodka in the middle of the room. I abandoned Karthik and tried my best to prove to Ameer that I wasn't such a bitch. 'Fine, you are not a bitch,' he said as we hugged when we were leaving.

Karthik drove me back home. We arrived at a junction where he would have to take a right to drop me off at my parents' place, and I thought that's what he'd do after the scene I'd made. Instead, he looked at me and smiled.

'Drive?'

I wasn't ready to go home either. I used my lip balm because clearly there was a kiss ahead. I was wrong, again. There was none. We drove on the near-empty streets of Kotturpuram and Adyar areas, occasionally stopped by cops who were checking for drunken driving. Women made up in rose powder and scarlet lip gloss, dressed in shiny clothes, their hair stuffy with flowers, stood in street corners, looking like I did at my puberty function. There was a photo of me at the function that I hated as a kid but thought of fondly now. My cheeks smeared with sandalwood paste, my hair braided with flowers, my mouth wide open, buckteeth on display, reaching out for a silver vessel that my aunt was giving me as a gift. One of the women on the street twirled in her ghagra-choli, right in the middle of the road, and I had this urge to join her. And then she bent down and kissed the road, as if in prayer. A little ahead, a cop asked Karthik to blow on his face, holding his palm near Karthik's mouth. It looked like they were about to kiss. Checking for drunken driving is not an exact science in Madras.

'I have this real urge to eat raw onion and come do this one day,' he said. 'Poor fellow. Must have cleared some important tests and studied like crazy to do *this*?'

We drove around. Talked about this and that absent-mindedly. And yet we did not kiss. In the end, I got a hug. And that was that. I was dropped off at home.

Amma was up, waiting for me. We were both in a better mood today, it seemed.

'So? Thaatha told me. So?' She was too perky. This date was feeling more and more like an arranged marriage scene. 'My father's being pretty brave with this proposal, you know?'

So this was to be an arranged intercaste marriage then? 'Proposal? What rubbish,' I said.

But Amma found another reason to critique me just then. 'You are stinking. What is this?' Her face fell.

I had a shower and tried to get rid of the smell of cigarette and rum from my skin and hair. I wore fresh clothes and poured some perfume on my hair. Still she complained.

'Why do you stink like this coming off a dinner?' she demanded.

'Ma, its 12.30 in the morning. Go to sleep,' I said and closed my eyes.

I could feel her gaze pierce through me, knew she resented my smoking even more than my drinking because she lost a chain-smoking uncle to lung cancer.

The next day, I was spared any further probing on this matter because my brother told our parents that he wanted to marry his Madhwa girlfriend. There was a new glow on my mother's face. At last, she too had arrived in the world of mothers-in-law.

'I am not going to be like some cinema mother-in-law,' she said to my brother. 'I will take such good care of her.'

'Ma, he is not bringing home a baby,' I said, and Nana laughed.

'Don't put ideas in your mother's head. Then she will start dreaming of a grandchild too. I need some time before I can accept my grandfather-liness,' Nana said.

'Make fun of me all you want, but wait until you have a daughter of your own. I will see what you want for her.' She was also a walking Jane Austen novel, my mother.

'Ma, I will be happy with whatever she chooses, if I ever have a child. Even if she wants to marry a girl,' I said.

Amma clapped back, 'See, you want to see even your unborn child happily married.'

# 15
# Rage

Karthik messaged to ask if I could meet him. I slipped out after breakfast. Amma was in a state of frenzy, dialling every relative's number she could remember and WhatsApping pictures of her prospective daughter-in-law in traditional sarees and modern clothes.

We met at the Connemara Library where he mostly worked from. He had permission to enter a part of it that was open only once a year to the public. On World Library Day.

The warmth of the empty halls bathed in plush red, deep brown, white and gold hues, and an otherworldly silence was comforting after all that excitement and noise at home. Karthik was looking for details about Old Madras's Paracheri, where his next story was set; a working-class detective goes looking for a long-lost treasure in the old shrines of his native city.

I found a copy of *Muddupalani.* Time seemed to have slowed down suddenly. I didn't think someplace this stuffy could be that, but it really was romantic, sitting there in silence. Looking up from the book every once in a while. The sound of a page turning. Of the absence of conversation. And of the meeting of our elbows, the holding of hands. The anticipation.

'Before you get in your car,' he said, as we walked back to the parking lot. And there it was. The kiss that had eluded me. It was quick, precise and held the promise of something more delicious soon. We stopped at the bronze gallery before heading out. I showed him the statue of an Ayyanar. A slender, attractive piece of eternity, very unlike the usual menacing guardian deity, sitting on an elephant ever so delicately.

'Some day, I'll make art like this,' he said.

'Then you too shall be eternal.' I held my palm up in a blessing.

We drove down the Marina because Karthik hadn't seen Robert Chisholm's wondrous world of red sandstone with someone who knew something about them. We stopped for pictures at the stunning grounds of Presidency College, which had seen shocking violence, but now wore a calm, nothing-to-see-here look, the Chepauk Palace, hidden away behind the new PWD building, then the port, the High Court and, finally, all the new metro stops that looked like they belonged, with surprisingly arty entrances.

It was a cloudy day. The sort of weather one needed to gallivant in Madras or you'd be toast. At the Marina, we finally decided to call it a day. We ate bajjis sitting on plastic stools on the beach, and spring potatoes standing by the water. After lingering around the beach for a bit, I had to leave to catch the train home from the Central station.

'It's late,' I said, 'I'll get going now.'

He got up and I thought it was for a hug, but he held my hand and said, 'I thought you could crash at my place?' His eyebrows raised.

'Oh.'

'I mean, if you are comfortable. Otherwise, I don't mind dropping you back in Chengalpattu.'

'That is a long drive and back. I mean, I could sleepover. If you don't mind,' I said.

'Why would I?' He grinned.

It was a cosy little apartment in Nungambakkam. Clean, but not clean enough. Artfully dirty, if you will. It was dusty, not filthy. There were coffee cups by the bed, but not so many as to stink the house up with new life sprouting in them. Funny how quickly that can happen. It had a small living room with an open kitchen, a bedroom and a bathroom. Furniture that looked imported, maybe from Bali. Indoor plants that were thriving. Some cactus in bloom. How are all these young people keeping plants alive inside their homes?

We had a few glasses of wine. He showed me the bed and then said, 'I can sleep on the sofa.'

I tapped him on the shoulder, took his face in my hands and kissed him.

'I was beginning to think you were never going to do that,' he said.

'You taste like candied fennel,' I said, and he burst into laughter.

It was frenzied and all electric at first, the way new touch is. We kissed breathlessly, clumsily, trying to figure out who should go where, and who should take what off. And then there was the trying to decide if we should keep the lights on or off. Off. It was too dark suddenly, and yet I closed my eyes. Just when I thought we were going to have sex in that rushed manner that would make the whole thing whiz past like a big blur, we stopped. And then we kissed again. Fennel and fire. Slower this time. Our bodies new to each other's graze, awake to every little touch. His hands, firm, held my back, and it felt as if we'd earned ourselves time. I kept my eyes open now, because he was exquisite.

He drew a map from a surgical scar near my waist to the mark from a fall on my knees. It was like an implosion. Except in slow motion. A language that was at once new and familiar. He undid my ponytail and my hair did that thing it did. Frizz. 'I've been meaning to do that all day,' he said, his lips still on mine. When I placed my lips on his ear, the haste sought us again. The sheets on his bed were soft, and in the darkness of the room, we were shadows studying each other. The tip of his nose, the coldness of his back, the pull of his fingers.

He made Maggi and we ate in silence, standing near the kitchen, nearly naked still. He held my hands every now and then, as if to assure me and to make sure for himself that the evening turned out fine. The next morning, I woke up to a light peck on my cheek. He was sitting up, fully dressed. I strained to open my eyes.

'I am not a morning person. At all,' I said, sitting up.

He gave me a hug before saying anything. 'Want to go see the sunrise?' he asked. It wasn't a question because he was now off the bed and flinging the camera bag onto his shoulders.

'Okay. Give me ten minutes.'

'It's 5.35 now. My phone says the sun rises at 5.47 a.m. today,' he said. His enthusiasm was charming and I tried my best to not sound crabby. But I genuinely hated being up early. Who goes to see the sunrise in Madras?

I stumbled out of his house to a city that was bustling. I was shocked the first time, as a kid, when I returned home at four one morning from the railway station after summer vacation and found out how early this town woke up. Vendors drawing open shutters, bathed and ready for the long day ahead, vibhuti, incense sticks and kolams out in front of stores as quiet prayers played in the background. Tea shops boiling milk, auto rickshaws up and about before buses and cars took over the streets, the stray black-and-yellow vintage Ambassador taxis dropping people off from the airport and heading back in a great hurry, looking ready to mow down anyone in the way. The air neither hot nor cold, and the possibilities of a new day, always endless in this beach town.

At Marina, the orange ball rising above the water looked calm and sweet. Not bearing any warning of how hot it was going to get in just a few hours. The light from the rising sun turned everything it touched into shimmering gold. It fell on his beautiful face, lighting it up. He was glowing, like a mythical creature. We couldn't look at anything other than the water or each other, however. All over the beach, plastic bags and cups lay buried. As if in a few years, the sand would be replaced completely by a filthy bed of rotting waste and plastic. The smell of shit was beginning to overwhelm us and sucking the joy away. And as the sun rose higher, it got warmer, and the romance of the sunrise withered away completely. He nodded when I asked if he wanted coffee.

He said, 'I want some cheesy omelette.' We had both at a bakery.

At first, I couldn't tell if I wanted to spend time with Karthik because *he* wanted to spend time with me or because I actually liked him. I couldn't tell if I was happy to just have someone ask me out. But it was becoming obvious to me that I was happy to be around him. To hold him. To take for granted the easy comfort of his company. We spent the next couple of weeks with each other. It was as if I was always a city gal. Not a mofussil chick.

I took him to all the places I liked to make sure he liked them as well. To a small art gallery behind Chamiers Road that sold works by students of bigger artists; to Sathyam and its popcorn flavours and set-your-mouth-on-fire peri-peri fries, where Lijo Jose Pelisseri showcased masculinity, repulsive and raw, and Mysskin painted fluid, moving frames. To delicate melt-in-your-mouth chawanmushi and tuna nigiri, with endless cold sake in Dahlia, karimeen pollichathu and cereal prawns at Marina. To the surfing clubs in Kovalam, where music festivals, rains and the beach made life seem bearable.

We also went to Valluvar Kottam every other day. We gathered by the park and shouted our slogans against the citizenship laws. Sang our songs of protest until the police were no longer friendly and the threat of a lathi-charge didn't seem too far.

The Madras we discovered together was one of promises and possibilities. Most days, the city was burning bright and we were ensconced in its heat and dust. But those few weeks of mist in December, raising hopes of a rose in your garden, were really the best. For love, longing and laments. At one concert, a beautiful, melancholy padam seemed to really affect Karthik. It was a chamber concert at night on Kavita's rooftop terrace. There was going to be a party after the performance. Coconut trees thrashed about in the wind in the background, and the sky was clear. A stirring rendition of a seventeenth-century poem. It was the lament of a man who'd been left by a woman. Without a microphone to distract them, the artistes seemed transported by their music. Challenging and coaxing each other, enjoying the performances of the others and that of their own. Always, the mridangam and the violin gentle, not overpowering the voice, the greatest of the generation's. Soft here, and firm there, yielding like liquid gold. I was reminded of Lalithamma then. Karthik held my hand and smiled, looking elsewhere, as if he too saw our future.

In a few weeks, I had completely moved into his apartment. He made place for my clothes in his small closet, and for my toothbrush in the cup in the bathroom. The first day after I moved in, he made all three meals at home, they were so-so, but we spent time in bed and binge-watched Hong Sang-soo, that was amazing.

I didn't know how to tell him I wasn't fond of cooking elaborate meals, and that I only did it for my grandfather that one time. I didn't want him to ask me to take over the next day and expect a feast. 'I am more of a one-pot meal gal,' I finally told him.

So we agreed on a system. I would make frilly one-pot meals, and he would make light, multiple-course meals. We ended up ordering in a lot anyway. And so our days were filled with biriyanis, lemon rice and poppadums, keema samosas, pastas, pork rolls, pachadis, kichdis and kadis, interrupted only by the making out and the merry-go-round of undressing, dressing up and undressing all over again.

I didn't tell my parents I was in the city, so I called them once in a while as if I were in Chengalpattu. I paid the neighbour's security, Kumar-anna, three thousand rupees to keep an eye on the door and to water the plants regularly, so I didn't have to worry about the house.

Things were going so well that I was not expecting to hit a roadblock just then. One morning, the two of us were out having brunch in Mahabalipuram, when a woman who looked like a model, dressed in a pair of white shorts and a white linen shirt, hugged Karthik from behind and plonked herself at our table. He introduced me to her. It was a family friend. Just as I was getting up to get some food from the buffet counter, her parents joined our table. The women had this buff, polished look about them that said, *I am rich. This is me wearing casuals*. Both mother and daughter had straight hair that looked poky. They were really good-looking. As always, I was underdressed in my dhoti pants from Banaras and a long, loose tee-shirt. The father looked a bit shady, though. He wore white sandals, and the only people who did that were politicians or those in 'liaisoning' work.

It was uncomfortable, eating anything under the gaze of the family. They were basically just eating leaves. Why come to a buffet to eat that crap? After some small talk around the table, Vinu uncle asked, 'So, Karthik, have your parents met?'

'Um. No, actually,' he said, pushing his food around with a fork.

'Your parents were very worried, you know,' Vinu said, looking at him.

'What's there to worry about?'

'I'll be frank,' bald Vinu said, and then he looked at me and added, 'Don't mind?'

I didn't know what he was going to say. So I looked down at my empty plate.

'Sapna … wasn't that her name? She was a pretty girl. And then she married that boy her parents picked no, finally—'

Rich bitch aunty broke in now. 'These days, girls are very *smart*, you know?' She meant something else but stopped herself and looked at me as she said 'smart'. 'This girl we know filed a suit asking for alimony without even marrying my friend's boy. When he didn't want to pay, she filed a DV case against him. DV, can you imagine? She's demanding a crore now.'

Karthik swallowed his food and made an indistinct noise. They were looking at Karthik, all waiting for an answer. I got up and went to the restroom and emerged only after twenty minutes. I sat on the pot and Googled DV case. Domestic violence.

'Why didn't you say something?' I asked as soon as we got into the car on our way back home.

'What could I have said? She is my mother's best friend. And they're old. You don't argue with these old people. You just let them say whatever they want, nod and be done with it. What's the point in confronting them?'

'Is this where you bring all your lays? I felt like a fucking idiot, sitting there, listening to him say I was gonna sue you for money.' Even though I didn't mean to be so acerbic, the words kept tumbling out of me.

'Hey, ya. Just calm down. He is an idiot. Really.'

'Are you rich or something?' I blurted out finally.

He just exhaled. No answer. I figured maybe he was. How did I not know this? I was even more furious. Did Thaatha take my 'I want a rich husband' joke seriously? Is this why my mother approved of him, because she thought I wouldn't cling to the house if I was set up with some rich boy? I felt a little sick and hated everyone just then.

'How can you be so calm? Did you hear what she said? *The yellow of the egg is really fattening. For proteins, our Indian dals are ideal* … I will eat whatever I *fucking* want to, unscientific bitch—'

'Of course you will. Why are you swearing? I am being calm, right?'

'Fuck you. And fuck your calm. I'll swear if I fucking want to. I need to go home, please.'

We didn't talk to each other on the drive back. What a waste of a pretty view, I thought, when we crossed the salt pans. When we reached his place, I packed all my clothes and went home. I felt like my eyes and throat were about to explode with fury, and my throat and lips burnt from all the cigarettes I'd smoked.

I went back to the old letters because I didn't know what else to do. I wondered if my ancestors too had a rage problem when they PMS-ed. At least I knew they all chewed tobacco. So we had that in common, all of us women.

11.1.1945
Madras

Dear Alamelu akka,

How are you? I am well, and am here in Madras visiting Subbu. We will both go back to Chingleput from here, as Kannaiya has to go to Calcutta for a recording.

I thought of you today when I read in a book at the Literary Society that the Nazis have been calling Jews vermin for nearly two decades now. I was very upset and wanted Hitler dead. I told Subbu about it. She told me to write down how I feel, since I can and she can't. As I wrote about my feelings, here is what I concluded—I think it made me feel better. I think you might feel that way too.

I think women must offer their love to anyone being tormented by evil Hitlers. We know torment.

When were we free? Not in our grandmother's time nor her grandmother's.

For hundreds of thousands of years, wars have been fought. For kings and men who play god. Like Hitler. In homes, women have cooked through all these years. Making chutney like Subbu is now as I write this letter. Or pickles for winters. Have women ever stopped drawing kolams because of how cruel life is? Women have woven sarees, written poems of love and separation as wars raged between kingdoms. Dancers have swayed in love for the divine.

It is our job to keep on living, and to leave a record of what we saw in our time on this earth. If war is always around us, hate is forever holding us, it is we, those in the pursuit of life's fleeting joys, that bear witness to the truth that art too is here. As is love. If hate and death are permanent, so are love and life. At least for some of us, some of the time.

There will come a time when all that is left of every man who thinks he is God are colossal wrecks, decay and sands that stretch far away.

We may die fighting you, Herr Führer, but remember, you too shall be defeated. By time and death.

I reason like this, back and forth, and yet my art feels like a distraction in these turbulent times. It makes me a bit disillusioned with my practice. With cooking. With drawing kolams and making chutneys.

I must ask myself why I want to sing.

Yours,
Lalitha

# 16

# Blowing Hot, Blowing Cold

That morning, I had another lecture with the first-year postgraduate class on agrarian movements. Karthik came to the staff room to see me. He'd messaged that he'd meet me there.

'I have a class now,' I said, not meeting his eyes.

'I'll wait for you in the library,' he said, searching mine. 'I have your pen drive.'

'Thanks! It has a lot of my work.' I'd forgotten to take it.

I held my hand out, and he asked, 'Can I read it?' The pen drive had the first few chapters of my thesis. I shrugged and left.

It had been two days. At first I'd avoided his calls. Even though I missed him. I sat alone in Poonga for two days, watching people, feeling irritated. I did not know why I chose the exact two places lovers flocked to in the city. At Marina, I saw men lying in women's laps and making out. College kids held hands and walked around, sat under the hot sun and tentatively, delicately got physical. I wanted to throw up.

When I came back from the lecture, my saree was coming undone.

'I'll just go to the restroom,' I said. I changed into a loose salwar-kameez that I had in the back seat of the car. After a rather unfortunate wardrobe malfunction involving my saree and a nail in the desk, I always kept some extra clothes in the car.

'I am sorry,' he said.

'Forget about it,' I said, feeling nothing really anymore, and we got into the car.

'I'll stand up for you next time. I'm never going to see them after this. I promise.' How sweet. I felt like a daughter-in-law who'd managed to make her husband agree to live separately immediately after marriage, like a sorceress.

'I'll stand up for myself the next time.'

In our own world, we were more alike than anyone else I had met. We liked the same foods. Our fingers, so similar, fit snugly as I slipped my hands into his. But the thing that made us the same, the thing that my grandfather too perhaps saw, was that we spoke a half-language that was technically too dirty for public consumption. A half-Tamil, half-Telugu that was tucked away like a secret meant only to be spoken with family. A Telugu existence into whose nooks and crannies Tamil had entered. Telugu was the language of love and hate inside the walls of our home. Tamil was the language of our world. Very few of us knew to read and write our mother tongue. We don't know when and how it came to be like that, but correspondence, even between family, and wedding invites were all in Tamil. Cousins who were more like friends, and friends who were more like family, we spoke with them all in Tamil. Sometimes, you spoke to different members of the same family in a different tongue, depending on your relationship and equation with them. And so, when people asked us where we were from, which is to ask where it is that they spoke our tongue, we had no answer except for 'here'. Inside this home. It is this insider-outsider thing that made us who we were. United by the misery of belonging to both places at once and no place at all. We didn't have a 'hometown' or a village, except in our surnames. Karthik and I saved each other's numbers on our phone as 'Vandheri'. A new Tamil party was using this perjorative that means immigrant or foreigner-squatter, that's us 'outsiders'.

The argument over what that random couple thought of me seemed petty in retrospect. Though I still knew, and he knew, that he should have spoken up. Or I should have.

On the way home, I told him about my grandmother's letters and what had happened with them, and he listened. He didn't let go of my hand, except for when I had to change gears. We were somewhere in the vicinity of love in that moment, I could tell. I told him about Saveri aunty's mild breakdown. Also, I had to tell him about the thing that complicated my access to the letters. My fight for this house that was eventually going to go to Saveri aunty and my mother. And my mother's hoodwinking of me, and the signing of the power of attorney behind my back.

I sensed something when I mentioned the house. A sort of discomfort. Maybe, I thought, it was too personal. He'd think it was all too silly, he was rich.

'So, are you rich?' I asked again.

'Well, I mean. My maternal grandfather is Muthulinga Chettiar.'

I parked on the side of the road. I needed a moment to process what I'd heard.

'He was a huge fan of Govindan thaatha's, and gave his second wife's daughter in marriage to Govindan's only son.'

I laughed because I didn't know what else to do just then. There's a story that Muthulinga Chettiar was so rich that the French took loans from him to run the government in Pondicherry.

'My mother isn't on good terms with her brothers, she's like, illegitimate, no?'

'Oh?'

'I mean she got enough for even my grandchildren to live comfortably when she was married off. But I don't think it's the inheritance she's after. It's validation, I think. She'll never get it.' He shrugged.

I had to go back to Chengalpattu, and on a whim, he said he'd come along. I needed to see my house, it had been a few days. Amma said to people I was like a drunkard in the evening, hands shivering with the need for alcohol, if I didn't see the house often enough.

'Hi, house, did you miss me?'

It was cool inside, like a loving embrace. I lay on the couch and stretched my back. Karthik came in behind me after looking around at the garden, and as soon as he entered, he scrunched up his nose.

'What is that smell?'

I got up and switched the living room light on.

I pursed my lips, and wondered what to tell him. I'd forgotten about it. When he came to eat, Thaatha had lit a bunch of incense sticks in the living room.

'You don't smell it? It's mild but it's foul, like something is rotting. I can't really figure out what it is though. It's completely unfamiliar.'

'Take a look around, there's nothing rotting.' I drank some water and switched on the TV.

# 17

# Banaras Again

After going back and forth on it over the next week, we decided to go to Banaras, where I would try to cajole Thaatha into giving me what he'd taken. And Karthik would sit by the ghats and write.

'Why don't you at least get engaged and go?' Amma asked.

'What? Amma, what is wrong with you?' I asked as I stuffed clothes into a suitcase. She was visiting me ahead of our trip.

'Two unmarried people going around like this. It's not nice,' she said.

'I don't care about nice.'

'I told your father's sister about you and Karthik,' Amma started.

'Why would you? What's wrong with you, Ma?'

'She will find out anyway and then taunt me about it, so I wanted to pre-empt her,' she explained.

'Did you manage to somehow lose to her again?'

'When I told her about his family … her response was …' She simply swallowed the rest.

'What?'

'Leave it. She's so venomous,' Amma said.

'You know I won't leave it now.' I stopped packing and sat on the bed.

'Her reaction was, *Ayyo!* Why, are there no boys in our families that your father had to do this?'

Amma didn't have time to dwell on this for long, though. A friend of hers who was leading a protest at Valluvar Kottam was detained, along with fifty others. She had to rush to a community hall in Thousand Lights where the police had kept them. I drove her there. On the way, she made calls to see if the police would actually remand them, or if they'd let the protestors go after a moral science lecture per usual. At the hall, she and the inspector played word-volley about the sections under which the protestors had been detained.

'That's not a relevant section,' she'd say every time the inspector gave her one, and he'd shoot back with another one. Finally, he admitted that he was waiting for word from a higher official. The protestors were beginning to get worried. Regulars didn't care if they spent a night in prison, but new protestors didn't want to end up in jail. They asked Amma if they'd be sent to Puzhal, and she tried to reassure them, unsure herself of what was going to happen. Soon, a huge crowd collected outside the community hall, and chants of 'Azadi' flew from outside the hall and inside. The inspector called Amma aside and asked her to calm tempers and to tell the crowd that had gathered to disperse. Amma said she could do no such thing, but that she'd talk to them and reassure them.

She knew when to chat and when to laugh with the police, and then she knew when to be firm. She knew when to calm the protestors down and when to egg them on. Protests had just touched my life then, but it had been a part of hers for several decades.

The next day, Karthik and I flew to Delhi and then to Banaras. He was a bit nervous on the way.

'He literally set us up, why won't he like you?' I asked.

'It's not about liking. Old people love me. It's just, I don't know, it's about him seeing us together.'

Karthik wanted to eat dosa at the Delhi airport. After nearly missing our next flight over shitty dosa, we made it to Banaras. I'd eaten two breakfasts. One at home. One in Delhi. Yet, by the time we landed, the flight swaying like an inebriated man near a TASMAC, I was hungry again. Thaatha was waiting at the airport for us, with a flask full of coffee and biscuits in hand.

'Why did you come?'

He ignored my question and put his arms around both our shoulders, and like a trio in a Bollywood movie, we headed to the car. Karthik got into the taxi, but we were both still out, so Thaatha nudged me and sang, *Kalyanam … ha ha ha …* and I felt the colour rise to my cheeks. I peeked in to see if Karthik had heard. If he had, he didn't show it.

Saradamma was happy to see me but her eyes were locked at the spot where my elbow met Karthik's on the sofa. He'd noticed it too. Between sips of coffee, he told me, 'I will make it stop.' He brushed his elbow as if he were sweeping her line of vision away. And it worked. He flashed a triumphant smile and went with Thaatha to explore the house.

'I can tell you a lot of stories, if you want, for one of

your books,' Thaatha said to Karthik as they stood in the pooja room.

'This spatika lingam, quartz, has been in the family for two hundred years.'

'One foreigner came here and offered two lakh rupees for the wooden panel at the entrance.'

It was like a highlights reel of all of Thaatha's favourite stories.

The following weekend, my parents, I suspected with intentions of trying to ask Karthik about marriage, flew down to Banaras too. They'd brought Saveri aunty along as well.

'What? I just asked in the WhatsApp group and she agreed,' Amma said when I caught her and Saveri aunty alone in the kitchen.

'Who will say no to Banaras? Gangamaiyya will see us when she wants to. It's her whim,' Saveri aunty chipped in, and then she winked. I knew it.

For a week, the house was filled with people, laughter and gossip. I felt bad for Karthik, for he was the focus of most of this happy gossip. The upside for him, though, was that he was being treated as if he were a son-in-law. The women were always playful, respectful, and the men acted as if they were a part of some sacred brotherhood. Amma was missing in action through most of it. She took Karthik and me along to a few meetings at the BHU campus where her friends were planning a few protests. At home, though, she tried to put all of that behind her to join in what was really the first bit of true frivolity we had together as a family in years.

One mid-morning, trying to escape the rowdy oldies, who were asking us whether we were living in, Karthik and I went to watch a film. Gopal dropped us off, and when I gave him money, he refused. Instead, he handed me money.

'I asked you to suggest a good phone. Not buy me one,' he said. I couldn't tell if he was upset, but he was stern.

'No … I mean, it was no big deal,' I tried to defend what I'd done.

'If Thaatha gives me something, that is different. It's the blessing of the old. You can't *give* me things, what do you think of me?' He left in a huff.

'I am guessing he isn't gonna pick us up,' Karthik said, shrugging.

'Is there a thing I can do without screwing up?'

'If we get a corner seat, you can show me,' he said, laughing.

In the movie hall, waiting for a rerun of *Parinda*, I recognised a voice from further down our row. Just as I cleared my throat to say his name, he kissed the girl seated next to him. I waited until they were done.

'Someone you know?' Karthik asked.

'That's my friend, Nikhil,' I said.

'Oh.'

'Nikhil,' I said, but he didn't hear me. Then the man sitting next to him tapped him on the shoulder and pointed.

'Hey. Wow. What's up,' he said, voice a bit high.

'Not much. I just got here a week ago.'

He looked at Karthik and back at me.

'Karthik.' They smiled at each other.

Nikhil didn't introduce me to the woman next to him. At the interval, he bolted out of the theatre with her and came in only after the film began. She was epic-beautiful.

Dressed in a block-printed skirt and a loose white shirt, chunky earrings, dark kohl and her hair loose. I was in the old, faded clothes that I usually slept in, and my hair was tied up like Naradha's in TV serials. Gah. Why wasn't I dressed to kill at this random rerun. Not for Karthik or Nikhil, but for when I met her. Why was I always going around in shit clothes?

When the movie ended, he got up, and just when I thought he was going to leave without saying bye, said, 'This is my wife.' Nikhil smiled. 'Neela.'

What?

'This is my friend Yamuna and her …' He looked at me and I filled in, 'Boyfriend.'

Him. Married. Now I've seen it all. She said a warm 'hi', smiled and left.

'Are you okay?' Karthik asked.

'Yeah, yeah. I am fine. It's … whatever,' I said and took out my cell phone. There were seventeen missed calls. I had switched it to silent mode but had forgotten to turn on the vibration.

They were from Thaatha's landline and Amma, Nana and Saradamma's mobile phones. I dialled Nana's number, getting into an auto.

'*Ma, Thaatha poinaaru, ma* …' He was gone.

It was not life shattering, really. When you live with the very old, they remind you that death is staring at them, or that they are waiting to die, at least once every day. But I had no time to come to terms with it right then. I had to deal with the immediate. Like giving directions to the auto to reach home and trying to remember the shortest route.

'I am not able to get through,' Karthik said as he tried to call his grandfather.

'They've blocked internet, and all networks are a bit patchy,' our auto driver said.

'Why?'

'Protests are going on, no? Today is Friday,' the driver said.

When I got there, I was greeted by a haphazard mountain of sandals and shoes outside. The house was packed. But in the courtyard, radiant, with the setting golden sun kissing his face, Thaatha lay in a glass case. I had not teared up and was proud of it until then, for holding back my tears in public. But that hard, cold glass encasing broke my heart. His two big toes were tied together with a small white cloth. He was draped in his white kurta and dhoti. Three neat lines of vibhuti on his forehead, and his favourite pillow under his head. People made way for me. I recognised several neighbours in the crowd. Most of our relatives must be on the way from Madras and Bombay, and some grandchildren and nephews from abroad. Frantically making bookings and flying long hours back to catch a final glimpse. Too many people loved him. Tears then made their way out of my eyes. I made no effort to stop myself. When my sobs grew louder, and I couldn't bring myself to stop staring at his chest, waiting for it to heave, so everyone could laugh for thinking that he had died when Thaatha had only been napping, I felt a pair of hands around me. It was Saveri aunty. Her face red and her eyes swollen with bags of sinus underneath. I dissolved into a puddle in her arms and she in mine.

I had seen him that morning and wondered if I should first ask him about the letter he took back from my cupboard. But he seemed busy and happy. I didn't want to upset him then, and figured I would ask later that night. When I left, he was eating lunch off a banana leaf, sitting on the floor, one leg folded and the other spread out, forming an obtuse-angled frame around his leaf. That was his typical pose. And that would be my last memory of him. Eating, as Amma laughed while serving him some food. He must have cracked a joke or sung an old Chandrababu or NSK song.

'He ate and sat on his chair and went like that. What a blessed man. What a way to go,' Amma said.

That's when I realised she had been preparing for this inevitability. I had tried to fight off every thought that reminded me Thaatha had very little time left with us. Even when he said it, I brushed the idea aside as if it were really far away.

There's very little time to mourn if you're young in a home where someone has died. There are phones to man, coffee, water and tiffin to arrange, things to move, including the dead. Hold his head, hold his legs up, carry him out of the box, make sure he doesn't break. Bring him out. Change his clothes.

Every day is death, and yet nobody prepares us for it. There's nothing worse than trying to go to sleep in the night, knowing there's a loved one in the same room whose heart isn't beating.

Thaatha was cremated the following morning. During the ceremony at home, before the procession to the ghat, even Nana sobbed, and I had never seen him crying. As the grandchildren walked around the old man, holding a fire lit with ghee, all of Thaatha's children wailed. But the worst blow came when the men carried him, resting on the palm bed, on their shoulders and walked to Manikarnika Ghat. The women, who didn't go to see that final all-consuming fire being lit, wailed at the entrance, hugging each other. I quietly slipped out and followed the men. Near the ghat, however, I couldn't bring myself to watch. I turned around. My sinuses heavy from the crying and my legs weak from the walking. There was Karthik, right behind me. We walked home together in silence.

I had missed a crucial moment of moving on when I decided to follow Thaatha. Then I was stuck in a limbo. The women had wailed and had a bath, and were washing the house. The men would find closure when they saw Thaatha's remains burn. I hadn't been a part of either, and could feel myself ricocheting back into darkness.

In the evening, I opened the newspaper to bloody madness. Nearly seventy activists at a protest Amma was to join, and couldn't because of Thaatha's death, were arrested and charged with 'rioting while armed with a deadly weapon'. Many of them were students and teachers and researchers I'd met earlier. They'd simply gathered at a park with placards.

The police had placed a photo of the people who'd gathered there in the local Hindi paper. A caption underneath asked citizens to identify those holding placards at the protest and to call them with information. The announcement assured them that their identity would be secure.

'Sorry about your friends,' I said to Amma.

'The activist types know what to do. They aren't who we are worried about now. It's the young boys and girls, especially Muslim boys ...'

In the days following Thaatha's death, I realised how much I had underestimated my own family. I had as low an opinion as possible of everyone. But, in death, they came in from out of nowhere and brought solace, the way that only the familiar can. All my uncles gathered after lunch near the courtyard. They left Thaatha's planter's chair where it had been, sat around it and told stories about the man. The first few were serious, about Thaatha coming through for them at a crucial moment in their life. Helping them emotionally, financially, with a job, with a match, with a phone call. But soon, as stories go, the ones that got the most applause were the ones that were about the many social gaffes Thaatha would unwittingly make, landing himself in all kinds of trouble. Stories about his sense of humour, love of cinema, beautiful heroines and playback singing filled the house, and at last I found a rope that would help me climb out of my misery.

Karthik's grandfather, who came in the morning of the cremation, had many outrageous tales to tell. 'Once, when someone asked him at a wedding, are you veg or non-veg, Kannaiya said, both.' Even I couldn't suppress a laugh then.

My mother spoke about how her father ran away from home as a fourteen-year-old. 'But by the time he turned fifteen, he became disillusioned with cinema here. He was constantly cheated by music directors who stole his tunes or made him play sessions, and never paid up. He joined the army band then, and was posted in Calcutta. That's where he came under the influence of communist leaders. A year later, he missed sambar a lot.' Everyone laughed. 'That's when he came back to Madras and started a union here for musicians to stop the thieving of art. Everything he stood for, for most of his life, he said he learned from comrades in Calcutta.'

When she was finished, Karthik cleared his throat. He went on to narrate how Thaatha sang the song *Kalyanam* to me, thinking Karthik couldn't hear it. Some of my more orthodox maamas and maamis seemed super scandalised by this indirect hint at a 'proposal'.

'You should fulfil his last wish,' Amma told us though, in front of everyone. And that's when Karthik and I decided to move in together. We didn't tell anyone else about it just then.

Over the next thirteen days, relatives and friends from all over poured in to grieve and console. They sat in the living room, where a large portrait of his was placed on the floor. In the picture, he had sandalwood paste on his forehead, with a thick kungumam dot in the middle, and that broke our heart every time we looked at it, reminding us he was gone. It was an absence that we felt in the air, in the home. The chair, the room he liked, it all felt emptied out. Like someone had snapped a finger and vanished. You could sense that a man was missing.

Saradamma was inconsolable. She had spent the better part of the last decade with Thaatha.

'I learnt everything he loved to eat. Who will I cook for now?' she asked quietly, crying into the pallu of her saree as she sautéed vegetables. She'd learnt Tamil for him. From him. The death was most cruel on her, because everyone else got a chance to break away from work and mourn. For her, work just piled on and on. I tried to help her a few times in the kitchen, but she sent me away.

'I don't know how long I am going to be here, doing this. Let me do it,' she said.

I spent the days sitting near the courtyard, hungry for stories about Thaatha. Everyone who came home had one about his ability to make friends. Or his letter writing skills, his music, his warmth … I fell in and out of sorrow, as if it were a cycle. Like sleep, it came, and when it had got what it wanted out of me, it left.

Amma and Saveri aunty, I noticed, were sitting in a corner and debating. It had something to do with the letter, I guessed. It had been eleven days since Thaatha had passed away, and this was the first time I'd thought of the letter.

I wanted to give her a hug, and tell Aunty that she shouldn't worry about this. My curiosity was not important. Amma was having a hard week anyway. She'd tried to intervene to help her friends who'd been arrested, going to the station in between receiving messages and people coming home to offer condolences.

This was a different city, a very different police force. When she tried speaking to a senior officer in Madras, he shrugged her off with: 'Even if *I* go there, I'd expect to be be treated like a nobody, Ma'am, you can forget about negotiations. Just deal with this legally.'

Wherever she went that week, her heart seemed elsewhere. At home, she was thinking of her friends, and at the station and court, during the endless hours of waiting, she was thinking of her father.

I walked up to the room Karthik was in. He was on the bed reading. I sat on the floor and bawled.

'When I really wanted to read the letters, I told myself I just had to wait till Thaatha died. How could I think that?'

'He didn't die because you thought that. He was old. And he lived a full, happy life. And he died where he wanted to. He must be happy now, with her, wherever he is,' Karthik said, kneeling down by my side. 'If your grandparents are both not here together, isn't that a sort of togetherness?'

'Maybe,' I said running my fingers through his hair. He'd been very helpful the last week, just being around. Available. I hadn't let him work on anything, and we hadn't even left the house.

'Do you want to go somewhere?' I asked.

His face lit up as if he had been waiting for me to finally ask.

'Yes. Can we go to the ghats? I want to see the arti.'

I called Nataraj, the boatman. He was happy to oblige. And so we set sail on the river and watched the crowd slowly gather around the steps. Nataraj narrated his tsunami story again. 'When the tsunami came, nothing happened here. Because we are sitting on Shiva's trishula,' he said.

'Not sure about tsunami making it here,' Karthik murmured, and I laughed after what felt like forever.

'There is such a buzz here,' he said to me. 'I can't believe this place wasn't even on my to-do list.' It was surreal because, elsewhere, the city and the state were bubbling over with protests, and here we were, as if nothing at all was going on.

He watched the crowd and the birds in the river, and I watched him. Falling in love in the quiet of the boat. I thought of the last time I was on the boat, how lost I was then. The high didn't last because I recalled the time I'd spent with Thaatha then. As if he'd read the fall in my face, Karthik moved closer and held me.

A troupe had come in to perform some bhajans. Tourists moved around, taking pictures and videos. Locals sat quietly, devout, asking the river for what they had come to ask of her. The ghats turned hazy from all the smoke in the arti. Chants of 'Jai Gange Mata' filled the air. We sat quietly through the entire arti and watched. It was comical towards the end. From the boat, we could see almost everyone in the crowd holding up either a phone or a camera, cocking their necks.

'Idiots. Can't they put their camera down for one second to actually see what's happening?' Karthik said.

When we went back home, Saradamma had packed all her things into three neat suitcases. Mallika wore a morose look.

'What happened?' I asked.

'I cannot stay here, ma. I will go back to my parents' house for some time. I have some money, it was given to me long back.' She looked at Thaatha's photo. 'He took good care of those who took care of him. I cannot cook for anyone else again. Maybe I will start a catering unit from home. He told me I should start one.'

That was the most I had heard Saradamma talk, and from her resolve, I knew Thaatha must have had a conversation with her about what she should do when he was gone. She was referred to Thaatha by an NGO. She'd been abandoned in Banaras by her in-laws after her husband died. The NGO trained her in housekeeping, and once she got this job, they went back to her hometown in Orissa and brought Mallika. There was a police case and some managing of the local police to do. Thaatha used some influence and got it done.

When she left, a sort of quiet descended on the house. Nana went back home, and many of the visiting relatives were beginning to leave. That Sunday evening, despair gripped both Amma and me. As if we were mourning extra, because we knew that, at the end of the twelve days of mourning, life would move us on.

I returned to the old letters for comfort. I'd brought what I had with me to Banaras.

30.11.1942
Chingleput

Dearest,

How are you? I received your letter and was glad to note that you saw the Taj Mahal, and that shooting will be over in another month. My father came to patnam last week and brought me to Chingleput with him. Your daughter is missing you and cries every day after lunch just as I am about to nap. I am glad Lalitha is here to take care of her now. She was always very good with children. I can feed people. That's the only thing I feel like I am good at. On some days, I alter the ingredients of some dish and wait to see that first hint of recognition or lack of it in people's eyes. I replace lemons with oranges sometimes. Jaggery with honey, and then I feel like an alchemist. Lalitha calls me Compounder. I am happy brewing my potions and presenting them to unsuspecting people. Nurturing, particularly the kind children crave, is absent from my bones. My mother was not one to nurture either, but living in that large house in Chingleput, surrounded by men, women and children all day long, I never felt the need to seek attention. I was happy, lost and insignificant. I enjoyed that. Our child is alone in patnam and I worry for her.

When he came to pick me up, my father said to me, you are safe because you're a little distant from everyone. When I asked him why he was telling me that out of the blue, he turned serious.

'We have been hearing rumours since we dropped Lalitha off at her husband's house after the last big fight. Of him beating her up often. And now she fears he has another woman somewhere in town.' My father's voice was shaking when he said this. That man just doesn't like it when Lalitha laughs, smiles or even if she's just peaceful, he thrives in violence, he said. He knew more than he was saying. I was able to make out from his insinuations. If I wanted more information, I would have to find out for myself.

Everything is the same here. And everything has changed. That is just how this house has been from when I can remember it. There are at least three dozen people for every meal, but their relationship with us keeps changing. This time, even though I am carrying, I have not been given a break from the kitchen. Amma says that by now I should be used to it all. I do know how to manage all the symptoms this time. The thing that no one warned me about though is the anger.

The rage that fills my being like the scent of burning guava leaves in the house on the cold, damp mornings of margazhi. My mother says it runs in our family. These sparks of fury in young mothers. She says it will last some weeks now, and will be back just before I give birth.

That wasn't the case with my first child, I told her.

Well that's a shame. You could have enjoyed a bit of that spitfire. No bother, you can make up for it this time and the next, she laughed.

The other day, I was in the kitchen when cousin Lakshmi dropped her coffee right next to me. Piping hot. Normally I would help her clean up. Or make her another cup, even laugh at her. Instead, I stood there seething. The room was white hot, even as it poured outside, and I felt like I was about to explode, break into pieces, and I wanted to crush her to bits, crumbling her bones into powder with my bare arms.

Why don't you die, I asked. I was a cactus, prickly, hot and thirsty, the heat swirling round and round like a dust storm inside my head. She started to cry. That made me angrier. I began to scold her. Even as the words left my mouth, I knew I was crossing the line, but I had no control. They just kept coming out of me like someone had unlocked an overstuffed closet. I sat down on the kitchen floor and screamed until my throat began to hurt and my eyes began to burn. My throat began to close up like it does when I am choking on my tears. I needed water.

When my mother came in, she had to tell them I was pregnant. All my aunts had come in as well. Then everyone looked relieved and gave me sympathetic looks.

'When I was pregnant with Bala, I nearly choked my father-in-law to death once,' Lakshmi said. 'I understand. You go to the backyard and sit. I will bring you some coffee.' How can women muster so much love for each other? Despite everything we do to each other? Usually, if I'm mean to someone, I'd feel guilty and not eat. The thing with this rage is, I feel righteous. I cannot apologise. I just move on. My conscience seems clean as a rain-drenched neem leaf.

The bad news no one told me, and one that I found out about as soon as I came home, was that my father's oldest sister, Kamalamma, had died. The woman was widowed just a few months after her wedding and spent her childless, husbandless life in the most dignified manner. If any of the girls in the house misbehaved before their weddings were arranged, their mothers, including mine, would not just call them names or heap abuses. They would also curse. 'You will have the same fate as Kamalam. Wait and watch, you little wretch.'

They said that even when she was right in the next room. We would try to take all their abuse in our stride, but that final curse would send down buckets of water from our eyes. No one wanted to be Kamalamma. Just a little after she was dressed up in silk and her hair was plaited with flowers from all over, her husband died. They took away any semblance of colour from her life. They gave her saffron to wear, and she could not leave the house to go even to the bathroom when she wanted to, because no one wanted to see a widow just as they were going out to do something. Most often, that great thing the men were going out to do was buying snuff powder, or going to drink in one of the other men's homes, or out to gamble.

She was, however, never like the other older widows of the house. If you were a young girl, you had no say at all in anything. Not about your food, about your education or your marriage. If you were married, you didn't have a say in the number of children you would have. If you were widowed, you shaved your head and stayed chaste. Something about widowhood had turned even the nicest of the older women into unhappy, bitter souls in that house. Every word that came out of their mouth would leave behind a taste of unpleasantness in ours.

Though Kamalamma had embraced the widow's attire, she hadn't given up on life. She would teach the girls of the house needlework and pickle-making, and she even sold her dried rice appalams to the neighbours regularly. She used her loneliness to liberate herself from the trappings of being a woman. She did things that made many of us envious, and soon enough, the women of the house, our mothers, too, warmed up to her, for she gave them hope. Women lived unnaturally longer than men in that house. They were all hoping to turn into Kamalamma and not the other widows.

With the money she made, Kamalamma would occasionally take Lalitha or me to watch a koothu in the temple, which is the only place she could go, and buy us something to eat. She would offer us a few annas if we awoke early in the morning and accompanied her to the temple. Kamalamma would also pay us to clean her room secretly. She was not at all fond of cleaning. She treated us to boiled peanuts if she couldn't pay us enough. They didn't even take a portrait of hers when she was married. I fear that I might have already started to forget her face.

The other big change in this house is most shocking. Lalitha has come back. At first, when I saw her, I thought she was visiting, because she knew I was going to be here. But when she went upstairs to sleep in her old room, I realised that something was wrong. I followed her. Just as our girl went to sleep, Lalitha came up to me and rested her head on my lap.

What happened? I asked her, even though I did not want to hear the answer to that question. I knew that I would loathe myself if I heard it.

How do I explain to you why my precious husband reeks of wild jasmine and another woman every day?

I was stunned. Why aren't his parents interfering?

Subbu, this is not child's play. She sounded annoyed and exasperated. Parents do not interfere in the lives of men the way they interfere in the lives of women. They do not care what he does when he is out of the house as long as vegetables and grains reach home on time. And somehow that does happen. I do not know how he does it, because everything he earns seems to be going to the older woman, his whore.

My Lalitha. Innocence stolen from her eyes. And her words.

What shall I do, Subbu? Tell me. You asked me to marry him. What shall I do? She was angry. Not a tear trickled down from her eye. I was proud of her, for that anger could be put to use. I held her.

Come with me, Lalitha. Come to patnam. What is the point of staying here? I kissed her.

I will take her with me. I know that I will be tearing her life up with my father and mother here, but what other choice do we have now? What the three of us eat, we will share with this other daughter of mine.

Lalitha said to me, after I came here one night, thrashed by his belt, my wrists aching from trying to stop him, one of our aunts told me, *you should have stayed there. Fix the problem. Why come here?* I am a refugee in my own home now. Her words were bitter, her eyes hardened and fixed on the floor.

I went and saw Father Francis yesterday, she then said, trying to change the topic.

I asked her how he was, and the monkey said, he's okay. He says he went to London and has returned with a weak bowel.

It was precious when she laughed.

Father said all who watch as the Nazis persecute an entire people, murder and incarcerate them as if they are all criminals, for no reason other than being born in a certain religion, must answer. If not now, one day. To their conscience, to the forces bigger than them, to death, and to their children.

Not god? I asked, as I thought about what she had just said.

Lalitha had nodded off. Perhaps god had too.

Yours,
Subbu

# 18

# Dear Amma

Later that night, I found my mother sitting alone in the room upstairs. She was taking a break from work. I asked if she was okay.

'When both your parents die, you truly feel vulnerable. Open, exposed to the world,' she said.

I held her hands.

'Funny. It's my father who's died, but I have thought of my mother all day, you know? Before we moved into the home I grew up in, my mother had little links put up on the ceiling for saree cradles, for when I had children. When we moved into that home, I was in class two. Can you believe her?' Amma was talking to me about her mother after a long time.

'As a twelve-year-old, I was endlessly fascinated by a plush, soft-to-touch, pink saree with a very elegant zari border that my mother wore. I loved hugging her when she wore it. I've always had a thing for soft fabric. One day, I wore that saree. Amma was in the bedroom and looking for something in her dresser. And I was lying on the bed and watching her when this saree caught my eye. I got up and asked Amma to tie it over my paavadai and blouse. She laughed and laughed as she dressed me up in this pink saree, and I was beyond thrilled. When I walked, in an awkward, exaggerated manner of course, the pallu moved this way and that. I felt so sophisticated. Amma wanted to go to the studio to take a photo of me in it, but my aunt was leaving town and I had to take her to the bus stop. I walked with Lalithamma, only half-listening to her jabber. On that walk, she instructed me to never call my mother first if I spotted something strange in my clothes. She said this over and over again. She said, call the neighbour aunty first. I came back home. And got my period for the first time, almost immediately, and of course forgot about everything my Lalithamma said and called for my mother.' Amma laughed. 'I have always been shocked by how Lalithamma knew that I was going to get my first period that day. Like a magician.'

She was folding some old sarees in the cupboard. I figured she was going to partition them.

'As a kid, my mother was very fond of sarees, too, and from her aunt, she learnt to make tassels. These tassels she then made on the sarees of rich Chettiar women in Madras and made some money, which she gave my father when he was buying the house. It wasn't much, she said, but it was still hers. That's why she loved our house. It was her labour too.'

Was that a jibe at me?

'The day she died, Amma appeared in my dream. I had been sitting all night in front of her body. Crying. In the morning, I nodded off a bit. And in my dream she came, standing tall. She was angry. She was chasing me all around that building I grew up in, asking me, "Why are you asking me to leave? I am not going anywhere. Won't you even give me water?" She was about to hit me when I woke up. And in front of my eyes, there she lay. All the men had been sent out, and my mother was being given a bath. In turmeric water. Her face smeared with kungumam. She was dressed in a brand new, chungudi saree. She loved Madurai chungudi sarees so very much. That is my last memory of the woman who meant the world to me. The woman I am afraid I did not do enough for while she was around. In a beautiful chungudi saree.'

Amma donated a pile of the stunning sarees, each one with a brilliant tassel, to me. I had to ask her then.

'Ma, can't you just tell me what this whole deal with Lalitha was about. It's not for my research, I can promise. That's been on hold for a while now. I need to rework it with Thaatha gone. It's just—'

'Why is it bothering you so much?'

'How did she die?'

'What!'

'Did they do something to her?' I spat the words out, nervous, feeling my throat nearly close up.

She broke into a smile. 'Is this why you have been so upset?'

'It just felt like something shady happened.'

'You ask any leading woman performer today about the kind of gossip she is the subject of. The things fans and detractors cook up. About affairs and favours. In those days, it was that much rarer for women and men to present themselves in public as equals. Lalithamma did. And she was huge, and so when she died, unfortunately, all kinds of rumours suddenly spread. She died in an accident. Everyone knows that. It's no mystery, but because of those rumours, we all stopped talking about the death altogether.'

I needed a few seconds to process this.

She continued to fold sarees.

'It's just—' I started.

She put the sarees down and sat with me. 'Just what?' There was something reassuring about her voice, so I found the courage to ask, finally.

'I am also curious to know what changed, between the years she felt so dead beaten by Venkatesan and then eventually turned to art. How did she get over the humiliation and rise to become that star?' I tried to keep my voice as low as I could. I didn't want to get upset. But it cracked when I said the word 'humiliation'. Because it was a humiliation I was quasi-familiar with. A humiliation that I sought to forget. Erase.

'This is why you want to see the letter my aunt wrote?'

'Yes, what did you think I was going to do?'

'I don't know, Saveri thinks you're going to publish some scandalous things about her mother.' My mother looked confused and relieved.

'I will talk to her,' I said. 'Why would I do something like that?'

'Yes, you should talk. She might be relieved to be able to talk to someone who cares about this,' Amma said. 'I can call her later if you want?'

'That'll be great, thank you,' I said. Was I becoming friends with Amma?

'If I do that, you'll consider a grand wedding?' she teased.

'Nice try. Is there anything you can tell me?'

'Well. No one owes you that letter, please remember this. So, if Saveri decides you don't get to read it, you won't. That is her right.' She went silent for a few seconds. And then made up her mind.

'You cannot repeat this to anyone. Promise,' Amma said, and held her hand out, like she used to when I was a girl.

'Of course I won't,' I placed my palm on hers.

# 19

# Amma's Story About the Tattooed Man

*Whatever I know is from my amma, who loved her sister terribly, remember this. I realise that Saveri and my father were each trying to protect the women in their lives, each cowering in an imagined shame. The two sisters, long gone, must be laughing at us from up above at all this drama.*

*Anyway, it was some time in 1942–43, I think. That's when Lalithamma came to stay with my parents in Madras. In '42, there was an order to evacuate the city. Japan was going to bomb Madras, they were told, and everyone was panicking. The owner of their house called my parents and offered to sell it to them. 'For a throwaway price,' my father would say, proud of the bargain he'd managed. The owner was moving permanently to Madurai. Droves of people moved back to their villages, selling their land for a pittance. There were people buying too. Hoping against hope that the war would end soon and that they would be rich when it did, if they survived it.*

*The Chettiar woman my mother worked for called Amma and settled accounts for the saree tassels she had woven. They were moving back to Devakottai. Her husband had sent word from Rangoon for her to move back to the village. My father was stunned when Amma showed him how much she had made. He called on the house owner and told him that he would buy the house. Amma gave him her money, too. It wasn't much, like I said, but it was still something. It made her happy.*

*During the war-scare days, they only drank dark coffee decoction diluted with water and some palm sugar. Without any milk. Everything was hard to come by. Even groceries. Amma said she cooked without any oil and dal. There was no mustard in the pulusu or rasam. She just boiled the vegetables in water. By six in the evening, a sort of gloom descended on the streets, Amma said, depressing her. Once she wanted to leave the light on because she felt too sad without it. A constable on his rounds blew his whistle outside the window and hurled stones at the house until she turned it off. The entire city was blacked out by night. Madras turned into a ghost city. My mother was also battling a darkness in her heart over her sister's marriage. She felt responsible for it.*

*Lalithamma, though, seemed to be getting better and better. She would accompany my father on his practice sessions those days and come back all starry-eyed.*

*'Lalitha slowly adjusted to life here, but I know it must have been hard on her,' my mother said. They knew Lalithamma was beginning to feel at home when she began to sing one fine day. That's how music came back to her. Like the call of an early bird, one morning, unforced.*

*Over the next couple of months, though, Amma observed something shifting in my aunt. It was not drastic. But slow. A very slow process with a life of its own. Lalithamma was a different woman. And my father claimed that it was all because of my mother.*

*'It was your idea to bring her here. She is going to set a fine example for our daughter,' he said to my mother. 'You don't have to worry about her. You are worried because you have made it your only occupation.'*

*My mother was not satisfied with this opinion. 'What did he know? I used to go the Chettiar's house and the homes of people the lady introduced me to. I had money of my own from the saree business when he went to his recording studios. That was my occupation. He thought I was going to temples. Men like to think only they can live uninterrupted private lives,' she'd say with a laugh.*

*When we hear stories of a nine-year-old married, or thirteen-year-old made in-charge of a household, we think of them a certain way. Like my grandmother and Lalithamma. I knew both women. It's not all 'oh poor dear', you know? They were more than their marriages. They had this ability to build worlds of their own. Limited-entry, invite-only worlds. Where they did as they pleased. They came and went as they pleased, and spoke, ate, walked, lived, breathed as they pleased. All the while aware of the fact that it was all brief; an incandescence. That it all had to be quickly dismantled and hidden away from those who sought to bind them. But they were masters at constructing these worlds that could be made and unmade at will. Even in a deeply skewed world, this was possible then, it is possible now. They were bound, but they were still people. Each with their own quirks, desires. You'll see.*

*It used to worry my parents initially to seem happy, as a couple, in front of Lalithamma. But my mother said that fear had somehow disappeared because the light in Lalithamma's eyes was back, ablaze. Since she started accompanying my father to the movie studios, she'd turned over a new leaf. At times, she even went out on her own. Even when my father was not in town. Her serenity made my mother wary though. And she was too scared to ask her where Lalithamma went alone. When she asked your grandfather, he was not forthcoming.*

*'Let her do what she wants to keep her head above water. As long as she is safe and returns home on time, without creating any problems for us, we must not ask her what she does. Do you ask me so many questions when I go out?' he asked.*

*'But she is not a man,' my mother protested.*

*'Thank god for that.' He was too calm, like he knew and wouldn't tell her.*

*When she told Lalithamma what my father had said, she too laughed and joked: 'I am better than a man, Subbu. I am a woman who will not become pregnant.'*

*'The cheek,' Amma said, whenever she remembered this.*

*Even when Lalithamma sang, there was something new in it. That childish eagerness with which she would throw her voice out had given way to something reflective, Amma said. The innocence gone, and in its place, a worldly depth. As if she had acquired a new sense of calm. Perhaps it was the distance from everyone.*

*How could anything that made her strong be wrong? Your grandmother decided that she would stand by her sister, come what may.*

*It wasn't just her voice though. My mother also noticed that even the songs she sang were new. She was focusing more on the words instead of just the melody, something she did not do before. My mother had never heard these songs. Dripping with the sweetness of love for the lord of course. They were songs of love anyway.*

*'Perhaps I was subjecting her to too much scrutiny. Perhaps she was just growing up and developing a taste of her own. After all, these were the words of Andal and Meera. Songs of unrequited love must have appealed to her in some deep manner,' she said.*

*This went on for a while and then, one day, the great poet and film lyricist Shyamalan came home with a little girl. At first, my mother thought he was there to meet my father. And just as she was about to tell him Kannaiya was not around, he asked, 'Is Lalitha home?'*

*How did he know Lalitha?*

*'I want to introduce Lalitha to someone special,' he said, pinching the little girl's cheeks affectionately. Lalithamma came*

*out. Her saree was not wrapped around her shoulders. Amma didn't approve of her coming out like that in front of other men, men who were not from the house. 'That's how it was in those years,' she said.*

*Amma moved close to Lalithamma and muttered, 'Pallu.'*

*Lalithamma turned around to the poet, showed all her teeth and asked him, 'Is there something on my teeth?'*

*'No,' he said, moving closer to her.*

*'Lalitha! I said wrap your pallu around your shoulders. I was not talking about your teeth,' Amma shouted.*

*The two looked at her as if she had said something amusing and laughed. Wearing an expression so similar that it felt like they had discussed her before.*

*'Why didn't they come up with a different word? I think we should rename every word that has another meaning,' Lalithamma said, and he nodded and laughed.*

*'How do you know her?' Amma had to remind herself to stay calm as she caught the accusation in her tone. She hoped he wouldn't.*

*'Oh, she came to the sets with your husband.'*

*Amma was about to go into the kitchen to bring him a snack with Lalithamma, but my aunt wouldn't move. She sat across from him on a chair. The two just looked at each other for a few seconds. And then, as if to change the topic of the secret conversation their eyes were having, Lalithamma pointed to his arm and asked how he had got his scorpion tattoo. 'You never told me about this.'*

*'It's a funny story really.'*

*'Oh, I thought it was tradition.'*

*'No. We don't get them in my family,' he said.*

*Shyamalan was sitting on the veranda of his house one day when a beautiful woman walked past, ink and instruments on her head in a basket. She went around singing, 'Pacha kuthaliyo.*

*Pacha.' Offering green ink to anyone willing to lend their skin for a few annas.*

*'I wanted to spend time with her. So I sang back to her, Kuthittu poyen …' Shyamalan said. She came in with her needle and mix of turmeric and greens, and asked him what he wanted inked. Anything, he said, and asked her what it would feel like. She laughed and said, like a scorpion's little sting, before inking him permanently with the tattoo of a scorpion. Lalithamma laughed as she examined the tattoo, sitting too close to him for my mother's comfort.*

*'I am here to ask Lalitha to teach my niece music. Paddhu has a gifted voice and good intuition. What she needs is a guru with a natural talent.' He said this to Amma finally, when she stood there unmoving, wondering what he was doing in that house. Paddhu came forward and cleared her throat and sang a verse from the Thiruppugazh.*

*'She was learning from Hamsammal. But I have recommended Hamsammal's name for a film. So she will be acting in it as the leading lady,' his speech was addressed to Amma, but his eyes were fixed on Lalithamma.*

*'I don't think I know enough to teach!' Lalithamma confessed. 'Hamsammal is a legend. She is a direct disciple of Dikshitar's students. How can I teach you anything after that?' she asked Paddhu.*

*Shyamalan rose from the chair and walked towards Lalithamma. 'You are very gifted, Lali. She will have a fine teacher in you. Do not say no.'*

*Amma was ecstatic.*

*'There will be pay, of course.' He smiled at Amma and left.*

*'He is a great poet, Lalitha. Or shall I call you "Lali"?' Amma teased her later.*

*'It is a very silly name, Subbu. Like a pet dog's, no? What will I teach that child? Hmmm. I am going to write down everything I know.'*

*Good, Amma thought, this will keep her home. When my mother asked her when she sang in front of Shyamalan, Lalithamma just smiled. That same silence that petrified her.*

*At first, Lalithamma only had Paddhu. But soon, Shyamalan started to bring in more children who wanted to learn music. At five every evening, my aunt would begin her class. She made enough to buy rice for everyone in the house every few months. Amma had never been prouder of anyone in her life.*

*Everything was beautiful in the house, Amma said. Many women, and just one man. The sort of house she had dreamt of as a child. The sort of house that made little girls happy and did not choke them into feeling inadequate. This was in stark contrast to how Amma spoke of her Chingleput house in her later years, she spoke with such hate. No woman was happy in that house, she said. Not as child. Not as bride. Not as widow. Never as wife. All of its women lived a wooden existence. Constantly monitored, constantly chastised. Always an object of sin. Now a vessel of pleasure. Then an object of disgust. Now a vessel of pollution. Then an object of reverence. Now a vessel of inauspiciousness. Then an object of fear. A woman in that house was not a person. Only a hollow being, bound like a kite to its men or other women. This is what she told me when I was young. 'If it were up to me, if I were to inherit that home alone, I would set it on fire to cleanse it of its sins, offer it to the earth for grass to grow and for dogs to laze. For elephants to bathe and rest. To the wandering nomads who come once a year, bringing ducks and goat, their tents about them. For trees to grow wild, spreading their roots long and far, without anyone to rein them in. On some days, that house was a snake about my leg. Or cuffs that bound my hands,' she said.*

*And yet, knowingly, Amma disrupted her dream home in Madras with the three women and Nana—a home that was nothing like the Chingleput one—thinking she was doing the right thing.*

*Lalithamma's year of bliss in patnam was about to draw to an end. The postman brought home a dreadful letter to Amma. A long, unhappy one from her father, her dear father, whom she loved beyond reason, for whom she was willing to do the unreasonable. She said she could smell his tears in that letter. Her father wrote at length in pain about his daughter. His Lalitha. He was unhappy that she had separated. He was unhappy with my mother for having brought her away from Chingleput.*

*'Had she been here, after a while, I would have convinced her and taken her back home. What have you done? How will she come back to this place after a taste of a big city and its many prospects? What will the family say of us? And what of the other girls? You are the only one leading a peaceful life. I hope you will do what is right.'*

*When my mother told Lalithamma about the letter, she did not flinch.*

*'If they wanted me, if he wanted me, I would have known. If I wanted them, if I wanted him, I would have gone. Things are best as they are, Subbu. You don't worry about all this. Whatever happens, know that you have brought me peace. You have changed my life. You know best.' Saying this, she went out again, alone.*

*My mother's fears at her disappearances for long hours, and my father's denial of information on her whereabouts, and, Amma said, her own cowardice, which did not allow her to ask her sister where she went, all allied and took the shape of a conniving, new will.*

*She could not stay quiet for long after that. 'If I have brought this on her, I will have to fix her life. If my father thinks that I have brought shame on him and on his daughter, perhaps everyone else thinks so too,' Amma thought. And so she wrote to Lalithamma's husband. She wrote half-lies to him. Half-lies didn't count, she said to herself. Just the way half-truths didn't. She told him that Lalitha was a woman lost without the love and care of her husband. That she did not know how to read Lalitha's mind any longer. And that it was best if he took her back with him, for only a husband could read his wife's mind well.*

*Amma told him that she thought often of his old parents, and wondered who would care for them and cook for them. She appealed to the son more than she did to the husband in him. And it worked. Sons were always looking to delegate their duties towards their parents. That was why wives were so indispensable to them.*

*It worked faster than she had hoped for. As soon as the letter reached him, Venkatesan had packed his bags and come home to take his wife. He stayed with them in Madras for a week. Thankfully, though, that week, Lalithamma did not leave home without him.*

*Amma thought she would be disappointed or, worse, shocked when he showed up. But her eyes betrayed no such emotion. She acted as if she had expected it. Amma could not tell her what she had done, so she took Venkatesan uncle aside.*

*'Let us pretend I did not write to you. Let us pretend you are here on your own. And let us pretend all of this never happened. Go back and lead a happy life.'*

*He just smiled.*

*She regretted it. God knows she did. We all do that one thing in life that makes us small in our own eyes. Something that requires someone else to forgive us, and they do, but we can never quite grasp how they forgave us. This was Amma's reckoning, a scalding heat that burnt into her being. She died regretting it.*

*'Why did I do it? Will they tell Lalitha that I had done it?' she kept wondering. 'Was that letter a bad idea? Did I send my sister, yet again, into the inferno, knowingly?' she'd keep asking herself and my father for years. And then, out of the blue, she started to get sick. She felt her throat closing, her chest exploding and she*

*would drop everything she was doing and lie down, gasping for breath. I think her guilt undid her.*

*To her surprise, my father was on her side.*

*'Perhaps you did the right thing.'*

*She finally heard these words from him in the October of 1943 when their brand-new home was flooded. They had to be rescued in a catamaran and taken to a friend's home.*

*'It's a good thing you sent her away. It's one less person suffering in these floods,' my father said.*

*My mother was mildly relieved, but still ashamed of what she had done. 'Will she forgive me? Will she find out?' These questions gnawed at her.*

# 20
# Only Questions

I had fallen asleep on the sofa again watching Balachander's *Apoorva Raagangal*, and woke up with a crick in my neck in the morning. I washed my face and went into the kitchen. Fruit flies had taken over a corner of the granite slab where I had left two bananas that were now completely black and slimy. I looked away and decided to clean it up later. Also, I had forgotten to put the milk away in the fridge. It had gone bad and attracted its own share of nightly creatures. And as I looked under the stove, I knew my house was attacking me.

'Why are you doing this to me?'

A piece of bread was stuck inside a shelf in between the vessels. In the past, I had always played the scared woman card and avoided any sort of rat-trapping. But Kumar-anna was away in his hometown, and there was no one else in the house. So, I called Amma.

'There's a packet of that sticky trap in the kitchen. Put some masala vadai or something with onion in it. That should take care of the rat.'

I didn't have the time to go out and buy vada, so I emptied a packet of onion pakoras on the sticky trap near the kitchen sink, bathed and left Chengalpattu to go to my parents' house.

They were throwing a party to celebrate my brother's wedding, which was going to be a civil ceremony. He lost it one day, looking at all the expense, and said he wasn't going to waste twenty-five lakh rupees on 'shit like this'. Without Thaatha to insist on ceremonies, everyone quietly agreed. The house was filled with uncles and aunties, and smelled heavily of coriander. On the terrace, some of my uncles gathered for their own little party with some booze, and Karthik and I slipped out of the house and joined them.

I'd sent Karthik up first and joined him only a few minutes later, because I did not want one of the older aunties to figure out I was going to hang out with the men. When I reached the terrace, Karthik and my uncle Sumanth from Texas, who was here after ten years for his son's mridangam arangetram, were in the middle of an argument. About reservations.

'How did you guys get to that?' I asked, and they both stared at me as if I had started it.

'I was just telling him you are now teaching sociology,' Karthik said, biting his teeth.

'Oh,' I said.

Sumanth uncle was slurring and embarrassing himself. Saying things he possibly discussed with his groupies on WhatsApp.

'I have a right to know if the doctor treating me did well in his exams or if he was a quota kid. Why do you think the private sector is so efficient in India? Just the thought of going to a government office or hospital makes me sick, filled with incompetent, corrupt crooks.'

Karthik was angry, 'Who runs the government, sir?'

Sumanth ignored Karthik's question and continued, 'Why, just look at the South African cricket team. They don't win as many tournaments now, do they? Its because of those ridiculous affirmative action rules. It is antithetical to performance and development.'

I kept drinking my wine, cowering in shame, hoping Sumanth would just go away.

'Look, all I am saying is we need a meritocracy.' He was rolling his Rs now.

'Oh,' Karthik mock-laughed. 'There it is. What do you guys want? A separate country for yourself? Is this one where you are ordained as high priests not enough?'

'Who needs a refill?' Sumanth mama shouted at no one in particular, and then went his way.

I spent the rest of the evening drinking alone with Karthik. We climbed up on top of the water tank and lay up there staring at Orion. I knew he was seething. I could feel it. In the distance, a UFO-like light emerged from the horizon, large and luminous, and the sound of the jet tore into the silence between us. I placed my hand on his, he brushed it aside and got up.

He started to leave, but then came back and said, 'Just who the fuck do you guys think you are? How could you just watch him quietly without making some noise at the least? And you … you didn't even ask me how my grandfather's doing. He took a flight and came to Banaras.'

I looked into the horizon, not at his face, utterly ashamed. He wasn't done.

'You're being an absolute bitch about that house too.'

Is this what he's been thinking of me this whole entire time?

'It doesn't belong to you, why are you squatting there like a leech? And why are you pretending to not smell the rot? What is so glorious about your past and that house? Didn't you hear all the things your mother said about the house and how it treated women? What are you doing there, acting like a fucking traitor to these two sisters who wanted to be rid of that house? To break it down and leave it for trees to grow?' And then he left, just like that. I let thoughts of Subbu and Lalitha fill the void of his absence.

14.04.1943
Chingleput

My dear Subbu,

I write this letter to you in great haste today as I desired to gossip with you right away, though you may read it only a few days later when the post arrives. I do miss our evenings, the hot cups of tea that came with carefree chatter in the afternoons in your beautiful home. I remembered today that you do not yet know this and had to write to you: on the day we left Madras for Chingleput, Venkatesan and I stopped at Higginbothams before heading to the railway station. He wanted to buy some books for his Mahasabha friends. Venkatesan found only one of the four books he was looking for, and you will not believe why Subbu. They are banned, the manager delivered this sentence like a blow, looking alarmed at my husband. I wondered then if the old manager would call the police and have us both arrested. I have since been having nightmares of uniformed men knocking on our doors and arresting us. I am not sure what these books are, but I would not be surprised if they have been banned for the crime of being dreadful, boring or vile, all of which are also his special traits.

The train ride back home was as comfortable as the circumstances permitted. Since you cannot leave the house, you may not know that all the big roads of Madras are deserted and the city is disconcertingly empty, as if it is a mere ghost town and not the winter capital of a great presidency. The bombings in Ceylon, Cocanada and Vishakapatnam have really shaken people up. The railway station though was anything but deserted. It was choked up with bodies, with the sounds of wailing children, men and women jostling, hawkers with pots of water and parcels of food, porters rushing through the crowds thundering 'Vazhi vazhi' as they made their way carrying large suitcases, wooden crates, even ripe old men sitting uncomfortably on chairs. It was as if all of patnam was there, wanting to flee. I was worried about you and wonder if you will consider coming to Chingleput even if briefly, if not for your safety from Japanese bombs, for our peace of mind.

Here, my in-laws seem relieved to receive me back though they do not say much. My mother-in-law, Lakshmamma, who used to be irritated each time I opened my shruthi box in the morning, and would lash out, 'You've started your sa-pa-sa early morning, before making decoction also', now sits quietly in the courtyard, watching me, wearing an inscrutable expression on her face, keeping time, and reminding me of the day she came to see me with her entire clan to fix my wedding. I wonder if she feels guilty, Subbu, for plucking me out of that familiar home and dropping me here in this cold, hard, lifeless one.

Last evening, she felt more than just guilt, I sensed compassion too. Lakshmamma, while drinking her evening coffee, told me about the time she was made to finish an entire serving of bitter gourd curry despite hating it very much. She was a child, all of five, and her mother fed her a small bite of the bitter curry. Little Lakshmamma spat it out and then her mother pushed more back in, and then she spat it out again, and her mother pushed more back into her mouth. This charade went on until Lakshmamma's grandmother showed up with an aggressive threat. 'If your father hears all this noise you are making over food, he will beat your Amma, you know that, no? You want your father to beat your mother up again?' The five-year-old quickly swallowed the curry, along with the briny sobs and gags that came with her tiny tantrum, because she wanted to spare her mother the beating. Even as a child of five, my mother-in-law said she had to keep her legs closed together always, never parted. 'Who are you inviting with those legs? Keep them together,' her grandmother would warn Lakshmamma. 'I had no idea what any of it meant, I was a baby, but just from her tone I knew inviting someone was bad, and so I kept my legs close together always,' she said. 'Braid your hair tight. Wear a red bindi only, not black. Where is your bangle? Why are you walking around like a moodevi with your hair open? Why are your hands and neck bare? If your father sees you like this, he will go bankrupt! No wonder he's in debt ... This is how we bring girls up in our homes,' she said to me.

And then, I think by way of explanation, of my fate and hers, she said the birth of a girl child immediately adds weight to a man's shoulder for he knows he has to wash another man's feet at the ceremony, her husband's, when he marries this daughter off. He knows he must bow to her future in-laws. Our mothers too know this, she says. One more girl, Lakshmamma heard her mother say whenever a girl was born. If only you were a boy, you could have lived like a king, she would say.

Lakshmamma was married off at seven, and her mother at three. Three years old, and married, can you imagine Subbu? 'The years we spend at our maternal home may have increased a lot now, but we are all daughters meant to serve our other homes,' she said to me. It is true, Subbu, generations of women before us have got used to their girls being married off at three, then seven, and now fourteen, and who knows, maybe someday at twenty-one, but I wonder if these hundreds of years of scorn, fatigue and resentfulness against us daughters will ever leave our blood. Will we also do to our daughters what was done to us? Will we ever be any better?

Encouraged by the conversation with my mother-in-law, I have decided to sing here as I would in my own home. She seems to not mind anymore. Soon after returning, I visited the bhagavatar; he was delighted to receive me. 'What will I teach this patnam-return,' he teased at first, but he has agreed to accept me as his student once again. We will delve deeper into voice training techniques that he learnt in Dharwad recently at a workshop. I disappear into that world for a few hours every day while Venkatesan is away at the temple. My father-in-law Easwaraiyya, if he disapproves, does not say so. He does not meet my eye or say anything really, except to ask for a tumbler of my rasam to drink every day after his meal. He enjoys my tomato rasam immensely. He too seems to realise, and this is a new thing for me, that we will have to get along if we are to live under the same roof.

Your loving sister,
Lalitha

# 21

# From the Very Core of the Earth

When I went home to Chengalpattu that night, it was hot. I poured myself some beer, and opened all the curtains to the ground-floor windows and all the doors I could. I slipped into an airy kaftan. Kaifi Azmi was on the radio. Chiding his heart. Ever-so-gently. Why won't you listen, he was asking. I went to him, curled up into a ball, when I needed to nurse a wound. This time, he had come to me. He was kind. That's what made this song so different. That kindness for a broken down, fragile sparrow of a heart.

*Rekhaon se maat kha rahe ho.*

I had a bunch of messages to reply to on WhatsApp. Most of them I ignored, but could not resist opening a message from rapist Kiran. RK wanted to know if I knew a 'confidential' gynaecologist. It appeared he had gone ahead and impregnated some unwitting woman.

'Did you stealth this one too?' I asked.

No reply. No blue tick.

Kumar-anna was back, laughing on the phone. It's a call he made at this time every day. I never heard the words. But it was always a light-hearted, gossipy, playful tone. I sat for about half an hour in the bathroom, just comforted by his voice. The occasional hearty laugh or swear word rang clearly through the two walls separating us. I nodded off a bit and woke up feeling breathless. I washed my swollen face and came back to the living room, and it was waiting for me. That low but unbearably foul smell.

I tied my hair up, lit another cigarette, tucked my nightie up to my knees and squatted on the floor. I'd try to figure out just where the smell was coming from.

Cheek on the floor, I squinted under the cupboard to see if it was a dead rat. Nothing. I looked behind the TV. Nothing. Went into the bathroom and looked under every surface, the bucket, behind the geyser, the shampoo bottles, the soaps and gels and creams. Nothing. Nothing in the kitchen. I hadn't even managed to catch the rat. Nothing under the mixie, grinder, fridge, vessels. I emptied the vessel shelf out and walked, sniffing. Nothing. I looked for rotting eggs, fruit and spoilt milk. Nothing of that sort either.

In the store room, I opened the cupboard and pulled out every single item. Rubbed every shelf clean with my bare hands to see if I had left some old packet of food out to rot. Nothing but oily dust. I then went back to the living room. Drenched in sweat. I emptied the cupboard there, with knick-knacks, relics really, ancient family history, all the while taking deep breaths. My hand caught a nail, some skin scraped off, I was bleeding, and yet, nothing.

I tried to move the cupboard around and look underneath. Instead of moving to the side, the cupboard did a little wobbly dance on its forelimbs and fell face down, the glass breaking into shards of terrifying beauty, threatening to cut me if I so much as breathed.

Throwing the cigarette out the window, I jumped, just missing the glass, went out and wore my Hawaii chappals. And then marched upstairs. I flipped the mattress, it was surprisingly heavy, moved the bed, which was lighter than I expected, drew every single curtain in the house, emptied every shelf, walked around the house over and over and over again. I still couldn't find the source of the stench.

I came back to the living room and squatted on the floor, in the middle of the broken glass. As I swept the glass, I looked closely at the floor to see if there was anything on it. Then I pressed my nose to it. That stench seemed to be coming … from the very core of the earth on which the house stood. As if it was something ancient. As if it had always been there.

# 22

# A Window Opens

I went to pack up all my things from Karthik's house. He let me in and locked himself up in the bathroom. Didn't even look at my face. I went from room to room, looking for my things, trying to scrape my presence out. Under the bed, my clothes, in the living room, my books, in the kitchen, my shoes. My lighter, charger, laptop.

'I heard from your mother that you're here. I need to meet you somewhere private, but not our homes. Can I come there? I know where you are.' She was hesitant.

'I don't think so, Saveri aunty.' I tried to explain to my aunt that it was over between us, and I couldn't have a visitor in his house.

I knocked on the bathroom door.

'She started crying, Karthik. May I please meet her here? She'll be gone in twenty minutes.'

He made us tea. Aunty arrived, the way only she could. With fruits and tiffin.

'There's kuzhi paniyaram and red chutney,' she smiled. I was glad to see that smile.

'I spoke to your mom. She told me you've moved back to Washermanpet. You're doing the right thing, giving that house up,' she said, and squeezed my hand.

Karthik said hello very sweetly to Aunty, and then didn't come out of his bedroom the rest of the evening. We ate tea-soaked sweet biscuits and drank biscuit-laced not-too-sweet tea. Saveri aunty's the one that initiated me into the 'dunking Milk Bikis into coffee-tea-water' business. I didn't rush her. We gossiped about my cousin and my brother and his new wife.

'I am here to ask you for a favour,' she finally said. 'I need you to find someone for me,' she said, and pushed an envelope towards me.

I knew what it was instinctively. 'Find whom?'

'You'll know who when you read my mother's letter.'

'You cannot tell anyone. Tell Karthik, I don't mind, he could help you, in fact, because his grandfather may know. But help me. I have lived enough years with shame that does not belong to me. It was imprinted on to me nonetheless.'

She left without saying bye to Karthik, she assumed he was sleeping inside.

30.12.1943
Chingleput

Dearest Subbu,

Hope you are your wonderful self. Here ... the less I talk about here, the better. This letter is not about here. It is about there. Where you live. Where my heart is. Patnam.

I am very happy to hear you are safe after the terrible floods, and devastated to read about everything you lost to the waters. I hope life returns to its old patterns soon. How scared we were all for you, I cannot tell you. I am glad it is all over now.

I owe you this letter because the dignity of your silence over my disappearances and your helplessness over my own silence keep me awake in the nights. My conscience swallows my sleep whole. Trust me when I say, I do not begrudge you anything for writing to my husband. Yes. I know. He told me. During one of his wrestling sessions with my womb. If I were in your place, I would not have been that kind. I love you, Subbu. And I thank you for your patience. Here it is. The letter that I hope will put to rest all your questions.

It was all new to me when I went with Kannaiya to see the rehearsal, to the sets, the day we arrived in patnam. It was a world so far removed from my reality. The artistes I met, the musicians, they were all lovers of cinema. There were so many musicians in the troupe that day, it was an orchestra fit for royals. I saw the magic of cinema as it happened. How glorious to watch a young dancer, bursting with life, throw caution to winds and act in love. I sat in a corner, admiring the voluptuous woman's bravery all day long. It was a long shooting session. Kannaiya was busy, so I was by myself the entire day. Around lunch time, someone tapped me on my shoulders. I remembered him from my old trip to Madras, when I visited the studio with Kannaiya. It was the poet, Shyamalan.

If my life were a movie, that day would be a musical interlude. We spoke for hours that day. I was surprised by how much music he knew, it was in his blood, he said. He came from a long line of nadaswaram vidwans. He'd given up the pipe for a pen. We sat discussing, arguing, agreeing and disagreeing about sound and purity. About my hatred of the microphone. His voice deep, his forehead wrinkled in disagreement and his eyes beguiling. We spoke as if we were friends. As if conversation was all there was to do. Nothing coy and no one on the set cared a damn about me and my conversation with a stranger. It felt like I had won something new for myself. Space. And the company of a human I am not related to in any manner. Not obligated to. Not expected to be of service to.

I did not want that conversation to end that day. I felt different just sitting with him. I wanted to talk to him. It was as if he'd heard my desire. When Kannaiya came to us that day, and just as I was leaving, Shyamalan whispered to me, 'Meet me at the Kapaleeshwarar temple the day after, five in the evening.' I nodded.

It did not feel wrong to go meet him. My heart was not aflutter. I was unafraid. I knew then that, whatever it was, if it did not create fear in my heart, it was not wrong. I went to Mylapore the next day and prayed to Kapaleeshwarar, listening to the mridangam and nadaswaram. He was sitting on the floor across the idol, his forehead without vibhuti, he is an atheist, in a dhoti and black coat. His curls swept back, and his nose pointy.

He took me from there to watch *Kannagi* that day. It was the first film I was seeing since Kannaiya took us to *Kalamegam*. I wasn't very happy with it, but the heroine's lines about blood and revenge, '*Pazhikki pazhi rathathukku ratham*' have stuck with me. I say it to myself, whenever I'm feeling somewhat angry, and add extra chillies to the chutney and think of my poor husband's piles.

While I was there in Madras, I wanted to drown more in his world. In this new place where I could be myself, independent of other people. In this new friendship. So, when he invited me to his house, I did not hesitate. I went to him. He played records for me all evening. Of all the great artistes he had known. Of records that were passed down to him. He can cook, Subbu, and really well. He made me tiffin, and I sat in his room with white walls and blue windows, inside that old house. Nobody there even wanted to know who I was, or what I was doing there. He played the veena for me briefly. Todi ragam.

After devouring the upma he made for me, I walked around his garden, taking in the fragrance of a new-found freedom. It was a home bursting at every nook with bounty. So different from any home I have seen or any place I have called home. Jackfruit trees that looked pregnant, wasps on nagalinga trees, mango leaf mulch everywhere, jasmine trails.

It created a sort of lightness in me, Subbu, these new butterflies that were flitting about in me. He was convinced, when I sang for him that day, that I must keep performing. His confidence convinced me as well.

The next time I met him was also at his home. I went uninvited, and he was not there. His sister let me into his room, and I waited for him until lunch, reading. His sister played some music for me. We spoke for long. She's studying to be a doctor, and is so sharp.

He came into his room running, happy to see me that day.

'I am so glad you came. I was thinking of you all day. Wondering how to reach you. I have to take you somewhere,' he said, and for the first time, that day, we went on a drive. We went to a narrow lane where music was everywhere, it was in the very air. In George Town. We ate that day in the great Hamsammal's home and then she sang for us.

When she sang *Ososi*, I cried as if I were a child. It is about a man who has left his wife for another, only to be spurned by his new muse. It made me, for a brief while, sympathise with my husband. Can you imagine how moved I must have been to feel that?

We went there often afterwards. We drank endless cups of coffee and spoke music and listened to music. Every artiste worth his salt was in that house every weekend. Some days, there was no talking, only listening to records. I felt life leap out of them and caress my skin. Salem Godavari, Kanchipuram Dhanakoti, Coimbatore Thayi, Tamacha Jaan, Manada Sundari Dasi. I heard them all on records.

I write this letter, not with tears in my eyes as you might expect, but with a broad smile on my lips, reminded of the beauty I felt in the presence of great music, of the people I was granted audience with. The songs that moved me were mostly laments. And voices that poured melancholy and playfulness into art the way it is meant to.

In this music, I found the resonance of those facets of life that nobody wants to talk about. About the things, most intimate, that can scar us, that can shake our very core, change us forever. And give us inspiration to live one second, and take it away the next. I learnt to sing a new song every time we went to Hamsammal's house. She was a great woman, a superb teacher and she welcomed into her fold anyone who displayed musical talent. I don't think anyone with enough music in their soul can turn away, having heard her once, without wanting to learn more. I thought of myself as a refugee in that island surrounded by those sounds.

He and I met a lot during those days. Whenever I was not at home, I was with him. One day, one of the singers on a movie set, a young woman, Shyamalan's friend, said to me that I must mend things with my husband. Her two older sisters were spinsters, and so she was giving me advice.

'Why?' I asked.

'Why not? You with him is the normal thing to do. I am upset that my sisters will be the reason I won't be able to marry. God knows who else is unhappy because you are here.'

I thought of Amma and Nana then. His and ours. When she left, I was still lost in thought.

'It's the idea of auspiciousness,' he said.

'What?'

'The thread around a woman's neck, it lends and takes away her status. Women can only be two things in our culture. Auspicious. Or not. A woman with her husband is auspicious. She's blessed to live long. To see a hundred autumns at her wedding for his sake.'

'Wouldn't it be better if I could ask to see these hundred autumns by myself? Why do I need a man to see those many autumns of beauty?'

The poet laughed. With him, I saw the world a little differently. I was beginning to think of my own self more than I had done before. When we went home later that day, he took my hand in his. And he stroked the place my missing finger would have been. It reminded me of that little white child we had seen in patnam all those years ago. It was not out of sympathy or a morbid curiosity. I could feel it when he touched me. I could see it in his eyes. He looked at me, my eyes, as if I was important to him. I was the receiver of all of his attention. The hours stood still and we were there, hearts beating, alive. I felt, for the first time in my life, as if I did not need anything or anyone else to make me feel whole. I was fine. A human whose heart was beating hard and whose nerves were alert and singing like birds that had seen the sky blush and turn pink as the sun came on at dawn.

That moment was it. That day, it began. We visited the homes of many musicians over the following weeks, and I started to foolishly hope that my husband would not come to take me back. But that foolishness was short-lived, thankfully. When I came back home to you, I admonished myself for trying to hide from my own life, my real life.

I knew that whatever I was experiencing then, in patnam, was going to be but a small part of my largely loveless adult life. I decided that I would treat it that way too. As I prepared myself to accept the fact that I would have to leave it all behind and go back, I also plunged deeper into that beautiful, sensual world of love, poetry, music and dance, ready to drink it all in and soak it all in for as long as I was there. What was the point of fear if it would all be over anyway? So, without a care in the world, I went with him to every place he wanted me to see. To temples, to cinemas, to the homes of his friends, to his other home across town. I dined with him and all his loved ones. I experienced joy then. Like children who meet for the first time at someone else's wedding. Who, tentative and shy at the beginning of the day, make new friends and, by noon, are running across the house with the abandon only children are capable of.

We had gone so far ahead over the months that he knew, just as well as I knew, that we would have to stop meeting alone the way we were. He knew that when, one day, he asked me, on a whim as always, to go with him out of town. To Mahabalipuram to see the waves crash. I wanted to, so desperately. How could I, without being caught? I then felt a small, burning guilt, something that sounded like our father's voice in my head said I needed to go back to my world, back to where I belonged.

And so, the way we came together, we fell apart too. Slowly, softly. Without the slightest of fears in our heart. Like the leaves of the trees in autumn that die, so new things can be born. We decided to meet only when others were around, so that the death of our friendship would not be too difficult on us. His many visits to our home to introduce new students were all that. A longing for something that could have been. And through it all, not once, neither he nor those I met while I was with him, cast a second, insulting glance my way.

The day my husband came to town, I was to meet him one last time in his home. I could not go. And he did not come looking for me. Does that not say something about our relationship? Something about him too? How nice it is to know that such men exist in this world. That some men can respect our decisions, and not come chasing after us when we do not want them to, even when we cannot keep our promises. Was it I who made the promise to my husband that I would deliver a boy to his precious family? Was it not the priest who blessed me to have a son and grandson? Puthra pouthra, did he not chant? Is it then not his fault?

I have come back to Chingleput, with my heart and my mind full of music. I go to the bhagavathar's house every day and learn new compositions the way I used to.

I am coming to Madras next month to perform a concert. I will stay with you, of course, but my friends, my many musician friends will come to the concert. They have been writing to me. They believe in my talent, and I cannot wait for you to meet them all. But I promise not to go off on my own, I do.

The photo I have enclosed was taken one day when he and I went to a studio. It was the photographer's idea that I sit in front, on the chair, and he stand next to me. I wore red hibiscus from his garden in my hair and he wore one on his coat. We took it on the way to George Town one hot, humid day. You cannot see the colour of my saree, it was blue. Doesn't he look like Himanshu Rai?

I write this letter to you because I want to tell someone else. So that my heart can find peace in the knowledge that I am not alone in this. So that you can carry this burden for me, as a favour to your little sister. So that you may understand what your little sister goes to sleep thinking of, what your little sister thinks of when she eats, every time her heart beats.

Yours,
Lalitha

# 23

## Storm. Calm.

I woke up gasping. Groping in the dark. Drenched in sweat, palms numb. I tried to make sense of the dark room. And then I remembered the evening—the secrets that came tumbling out of its womb, my sleep in which several seemingly unrelated dreams melted into each other, flashing by so fast that I could no longer make sense of what was happening. I felt as if I had woken up not on the same day after falling asleep at the dining table, reading the letter, but a year or so later.

In the bathroom mirror, a pair of defiant eyes stared back at me. I wanted to fix things with Karthik, but didn't know how to. There was no manual to being a free woman. Or doing the right thing by love. I avoided looking into those puffy, cloudy eyes.

I made myself a cup of coffee. I heard Karthik in his room. No words passed between us. I dug deep and still couldn't find the right ones. A violent wind sent the wooden windows slapping. It was dark outside, a sudden cloud had assembled. And then it poured. A stubborn, wooden, pointy rain that pierced me when I put my hand out of the window.

A violent cleansing ensued. Leaves, branches, people, tarpaulin. It felt like the end of the world. As if all of life would end by the time the downpour was done washing away the dirt in our souls. As if life was this and now. And there would be no more. I was not sure if I could drive all the way back home until it stopped, water was steadily rising on the streets, it was already knee-high. Karthik came to see the rain, and stood next to me by the window. From somewhere deep within, I found my voice at last.

'You think I'm stuck here?'

In my dream, young Lalitha asked her tall, beautiful man this question. Her eyes defiant, as if she knew the answer already but she was daring him to tell her, anyway.

'Only if you want to be.'